Several shapes materialized amid the London fog

They were male, but several wore eye shadow and rouge. A few had dyed their hair purple or green. Two of them wore safety pins for earrings. All of them sported chains and studded belts and jackets.

"Hell," Calvin James muttered to his Phoenix Force colleagues as a beefy hood with purple spiked hair stepped forward.

"You fellas had best not give us any trouble," the punk said as he unwound a chain from around his waist.

"You guys don't know what trouble is," Encizo remarked.

"Look, you bastards can either hand everything over without a struggle, or we'll do this the hard way," snarled the troublemaker.

"Hard for you, boy," Katz warned. "If you take one more step, I'll kill you."

The kid whirled to face Katz. The Israeli had extended his right arm and pointed a gloved index finger at the young thug.

The punk laughed at this absurd gesture. "You senile old bastard," he snorted as he swung the chain and started toward Katz. "I'm going to teach you...."

Orange flame burst from the tip of Katz's finger.

Mack Bolan's

PHOENIX FORCE

PHOENIX FORCE

The Viper Factor

Gar Wilson

A GOLD EAGLE BOOK FROM
W🌐RLDWIDE

TORONTO · NEW YORK · LONDON · PARIS
AMSTERDAM · STOCKHOLM · HAMBURG
ATHENS · MILAN · TOKYO · SYDNEY

First edition January 1985

ISBN 0-373-61315-6

Special thanks and acknowledgment to
William Fieldhouse for his contributions to this work.

Printed in Canada

1

Private First Class Thomas Griffin approached the mannequin. Weird shit going on, he thought. Whoever heard of dressing up department store dummies in U.S. Army uniforms and taking them on a field exercise? Sometimes Griffin figured the United States Army was goddamn nuts.

Griffin's outfit, the 510 Infantry Battalion, had set up camp in a so-called forest in South Carolina. It seemed as though most of the forests in the state wanted to be jungles. No wonder the Army had chosen the area for Fort Jackson.

One of the largest military bases in the United States, Fort Jackson had everything necessary to make a recruit's life miserable, Griffin thought. It had swamps, complete with quicksand, sadistic plant life with needle-like thorns and deerflies that collected more GI blood than the Red Cross.

Fort Jackson also had fire ants and poisonous snakes. And last but not least, Fort Jackson had the infamous Drag Ass Hill—Nature's version of an obstacle course. Any part of a trainee's body could get broken on Drag Ass Hill, up to and including his balls.

The Five-ten had been sent into the field for a war game. It was supposed to be something special, but the military made everything sound as if it was a matter of global importance. Griffin just hoped they would not have to practice Escape and Evasion. He was terrified of getting lost in the swamps.

This, however, was a little different than your average war game. Everyone had been issued sixty rounds of blank ammo for their M-16 assault rifles. They had been told to watch for aggressors. But what the hell were the dummies for?

Two mannequins had been positioned at the perimeter of the bivouac area. Another had been set on a platform at the top of a thirty-foot tree. The last dummy was placed inside a GP medium tent all by itself. That one was dressed in an OD uniform with a silver general's star tacked to its green baseball cap. Weird shit.

Griffin stared at the frozen plastic features of the mannequin at the edge of the campsite and grinned as he reached into a pocket and removed a black laundry marker. Griffin glanced about to be certain no one was watching. Twilight had fallen, but the darkness was not dense yet. Griffin raised the marker and drew the felt tip under the nose of the mannequin.

He marked a small black Hitler mustache on the dummy's upper lip. Griffin raised the marker and drew a single vertical bar on the cap perched on the dummy's head, then stepped back and admired his handiwork as best he could in the dim light. He wondered if First Lieutenant Snider would appreciate the symbolic meaning of this gesture.

Suddenly, an object shot through the shadows. The missile hissed as it hurtled past the startled soldier. Griffin gasped. The projectile slammed into the mannequin, and Griffin was suddenly staring at a slender eight-inch shaft protruding from the upper torso of the dummy.

"Holy shit," Griffin rasped.

Without warning Griffin was seized from behind. A hand clamped over his mouth as his assailant bent him backward. Griffin felt an index finger slide across his throat from one ear to the other.

"I just cut your throat, *chico*," a voice whispered. "You're out of the game."

The assailant released Griffin, and the soldier turned to see a muscular figure dressed in a black night-camouflage uniform. Even, white teeth smiled at Griffin. The stranger's swarthy, handsome face seemed friendly despite the circumstances.

"Come on," Rafael Encizo insisted. "You and Lieutenant Hitler bought the farm. Now get down on the ground and play dead."

Encizo watched the young soldier reluctantly follow the command. A seasoned veteran of clandestine combat, Encizo had formerly been a Cuban freedom fighter and had paid his dues in the Bay of Pigs invasion. He was held prisoner in Castro's El Principe. He was beaten, starved and tortured. But he endured the suffering without betraying his friends.

The Cuban warrior had killed a prison guard with his bare hands and successfully escaped to the United States. Encizo continued to fight the Devil regardless of what form the horned bastard assumed—Communist agents, terrorists or heroin smugglers.

Very few men could equal Encizo's experience and expertise as a covert warrior and antiterrorist. Four of his peers were also members of Phoenix Force, the best fighting unit of international ass-kickers ever assembled to combat tyranny and terrorism throughout the world.

David McCarter, another superpro of Phoenix Force, lurked in the bushes at the edge of the camp. The tall, fox-faced British commando had formerly served in the elite Special Air Service. He had seen action in Vietnam, Oman, Hong Kong and his native Great Britain before he joined Phoenix Force. McCarter lived for combat. He felt more at home on the battlefield than in his old neighborhood in the East End of London.

The Briton worked the cocking mechanism of his Barnett Commando crossbow and placed another bolt in the grooved frame. He braced the skeletal stock against his shoulder and peered through the Starlite nightscope.

McCarter aimed carefully and squeezed the trigger. The bowstring sang as it released the bolt. McCarter saw the shaft of the quarrel jut from the chest of the mannequin on the platform at the treetop. He smiled with satisfaction and laid down the Barnett.

Another soldier heard the twang of the crossbow and advanced toward the bushes, uncertain what the sound might be. He unslung his M-16 from his shoulder and reached for the ammo pouch on his belt to draw a magazine.

Suddenly, a hand seized his collar and yanked him backward. A hard object was jammed under his jawbone. The trooper moaned softly, unable to utter a louder sound.

"You're dead, soldier," a voice whispered at his ear. "I just ripped your throat out with this."

The metal object moved from the trooper's jaw, and a prosthetic device with three steel hooks rose up in front of the man's face. The hooks snapped together like a bear trap. The soldier stared at the points of the curved blades. He swallowed hard.

"Get down and stay down," the assailant instructed. "Don't forget, you're dead."

The soldier obeyed. He glanced up at his opponent and his mouth fell open with surprise when he saw that his attacker was a slightly paunchy, middle-aged man with iron-gray hair and gentle blue eyes. His sympathetic smile was a startling contrast to the wicked-looking prosthesis that jutted from his right sleeve.

"Don't feel bad about this," the man said softly. "You can learn from mistakes in a war game so they won't cost your life when the real thing happens."

Colonel Yakov Katzenelenbogen stepped over the youth and headed toward the bushes. The battle-hardened Israeli was the unit commander of Phoenix Force. Few men have lived to acquire as much experience in combat, espionage and commando tactics as Katz. Few have suffered as much at the hands of the human monsters that stalk the earth.

Animals that wore jackboots and swastikas had murdered most of Katz's family in France. Already an accomplished linguist who spoke French, German, Russian and English fluently, the young Yakov fought the Nazis and participated in missions with the Resistance and the American OSS.

The Third Reich was crushed at the end of World War II, but Katz moved from one conflict to another when he traveled to Palestine and joined the war for independence of the Jewish state of Israel. This goal was eventually achieved, yet the endless struggle with neighboring Arab nations continued.

Katz lost his right arm and his only son during the Six Day War with Egypt. Yet Katz knew intimately the horror and devastation that had become part of life in the Middle East. Atrocities were committed by both sides.

Katz served in the Israeli Mossad intelligence organization and he later carried out a few missions for the American CIA in Europe. Then he was recruited by Phoenix Force. For Colonel Yakov Katzenelenbogen, it was the perfect position in life, doing what he did best.

PRIVATE SECOND CLASS ROBERT COLE was on guard duty on the opposite side of the camp. He patroled the perimeter, unaware that the bivouac area was under assault. Then out of the corner of his eye he saw something move. He turned sharply as a rigid humanoid figure fell to the ground.

"What the hell . . . ?" Cole rasped through clenched teeth.

He approached cautiously, fumbling for a magazine from an ammo pouch. Cole almost wished he had live rounds instead of blanks. Training exercise or not, he still thought he had seen a man's body fall dead before his eyes.

"Shit," he said and chuckled when he gazed down at the mannequin that lay on the ground. "Damn thing fell over."

Then he noticed a steel dart lodged in the plastic forehead of the dummy. The projectile had struck the mannequin right between its glass eyes. Cole backed away from the inert figure, as terrified as he would have been if he had discovered a genuine corpse.

A hard object pressed between his shoulder blades. Cole stiffened. He dropped the M-16 and raised his hands in surrender. God, Cole thought. Please let this be one of the guys bullshitting around and not some crazy hillbilly with a grudge against servicemen.

"Don't panic," a voice urged. "If this was for real, you'd already be dead."

"You . . . you shot the dummy, sir?" Cole stammered.

He was still frightened. Christ, the dude had crept up behind him like a cat. Who the hell were these aggressors? Apaches?

"Yeah," the voice confirmed. "I shot the mannequin. Used an Anschutz 22-caliber air rifle with an infrared scope. Silent and no muzzle-flash. Now, play dead and let me get back to business, son.''

Cole was too nervous to even glance over his shoulder at the mysterious aggressor. If he had, Cole would have seen a rugged muscular man with dark blond hair, a stern poker face and gunmetal-gray eyes.

Gary Manning was a serious man, a hard-nosed workaholic with exceptional physical and mental endurance. The Canadian member of Phoenix Force was an explosives expert and a superb rifle marksman. He had practiced his deadly skills in Vietnam and with antiterrorist units in Canada and West Germany.

Manning had dedicated his life to fighting the disciples of slavery and destruction. His bulldog determination and workhorse strength were matched only by his skill and courage.

After subduing the guard, the Canadian moved deeper into the campsite. He kept in the shadows as he hurried to a tree trunk for cover. His instincts had been honed by years of hunting deer in the Canadian woods and men in every conceivable environment. This sixth sense warned him in time to avoid discovery as two disgruntled soldiers shuffled toward a ring of sandbags. The pair walked right past Manning's position, unaware of the Canadian's presence.

"This is bullshit, man," one of the soldiers complained as he hauled a heavy M-60 machine gun to the sandbags. "Setting up this goddamn thing is taking this war game crap too damn far."

"So bitch to Major Strothers," his companion replied. "This is his idea, not mine, Joey."

"Hell," Joey muttered. "Figure we should load this sucker now, Dan?"

"Why not?" The second trooper shrugged, opening a metal ammunition case. He removed a long belt of

7.62mm cartridges. ''That's what we got this ammo for.''

''Hey, are you sure that's all blank rounds?'' Joey asked as he braced the M-60 bipod against the sandbags.

''You were there when we checked the cartridges,'' Dan replied. ''We checked them three times to be one-hundred-percent sure. It's all blank ammo, man. Not a joker in the deck.''

''Okay.'' Joey nodded. ''Let's load this mother!''

A harsh metallic cough startled the pair. They turned to see a dark shape seated on the sandbags behind them. A tall, slender, black man, dressed in night-combat uniform, smiled at the soldiers. He held a .45-caliber Colt Commander in his fist. A nine-inch sound suppressor was attached to the muzzle.

''Hi,'' he greeted. ''I'm an aggressor and you guys are both dead.''

He pointed the Colt at the night sky and squeezed the trigger. Another muffled shot burst from the silenced pistol.

''Okay,'' the black man explained, ''I could have shot one of you in the back of the head before you dudes even knew I was here. When the other guy turned around, I would have pumped a bullet into his heart. Man, you dudes are lucky this is just a game.''

''Uh. . . yes, sir,'' Joey replied woodenly nodding his head.

Calvin James looked at the two soldiers. James was the newest addition to Phoenix Force. Although younger than his four teammates, he had a background as a fighter that began with his childhood in the south side of Chicago. He had used his fists and feet in street fights and later learned to handle a knife and chain as weapons. Yet his worst opponent of all could not be beaten in hand-to-hand combat. James discovered early that poverty can only be defeated by determination and hard work.

James joined the Navy when he was seventeen and became a hospital corpsman. He later became a member of the elite SEALs and saw a new kind of combat in a different kind of jungle called Vietnam. After the war he joined another elite unit, the San Francisco SWAT team. Although he received praise and honors for his courage and exceptional performance while a member of both groups, James had never really fit in with any organization that followed strict rules and regulations.

Calvin James was a perfect choice for Phoenix Force. His abilities as a medic, chemist, frogman and a veteran of both jungle and urban warfare all made him ideal to serve with the five-man army. James had finally found his place in life.

"Looks like you've got this situation taken care of," Gary Manning whispered as he materialized beside the black man. "Need any help with that M-60?"

"I can manage," James assured his partner. "Okay, you two dead guys, get out of my foxhole."

SERGEANT FIRST CLASS JOHN THOMPSON emerged from a tent. The mess sergeant for Bravo Company, Thompson had seen action in Vietnam. He recalled the haunting sensation of fear that had warned the veteran survivalist of danger in the jungle. That same feeling was knotting up his stomach once more.

But Vietnam had been more than a decade ago. The present mission was just a training exercise in the good old U.S. of A. It was silly to be frightened during a goddamn war game. The aggressors were only acting out a role and all the guns were loaded with blank ammo. An adult version of Cowboys and Indians.

"Damn it," Thompson whispered. "Something is out there."

The NCO saw nothing sinister and heard nothing to suggest the camp was under siege. Yet that knot would not go away. He felt the presence of a warrior force. Invisible Viking spirits from Valhalla surrounded the campsite.

Suddenly, objects hurtled through the night sky. One landed near Thompson. It was a green canister. Billows of smoke immediately spewed from the grenade.

"Aw, shit," the sergeant muttered. "I'm dead."

Green smoke filled the camp as more grenades erupted. Soldiers burst from tents. Most failed to grab their M-16s as they fled. Officers and noncoms shouted orders. Men groaned and cursed as they ran into each other in the dense artificial fog.

Some managed to reach the perimeters of the camp, where they found Phoenix Force waiting for them. Calvin James fired the M-60 machine gun from his foxhole at the west side of the camp. Katz waited at the east, an Uzi submachine gun braced along his prosthesis spitting fire at the terrified troopers.

Gary Manning, positioned at the south end, had abandoned his air rifle and armed himself with a Heckler & Koch MP5A3 subgun. He held the weapon in one hand and fired blank ammo at the soldiers while he pressed down the plunger of a detonator with the other.

Firecrackerlike explosions burst at the bases of several trees within the campsite. Completely disoriented, soldiers threw down their weapons and dived to the ground, covering their heads with their arms. This can't be real, they thought. But they ducked just in case.

David McCarter and Rafael Encizo advanced from the north. The British commando fired an Ingram M-10 machine pistol as he ran. Encizo held a Smith & Wesson M-76 submachine gun in his fists. He triggered several 3-round bursts of 9mm blanks as the pair raced to the center of the camp.

McCarter plunged through the canvas flap of a tent and exhausted the blank ammo from the magazine of his Ingram. Encizo followed. The M-76 in his left fist, the Cuban drew a Gerber Mark I fighting dagger with his right.

The Gerber struck home. The steel tip punctured cloth and plastic, and the mannequin tipped over with the knife lodged in its chest. A cap bearing a silver star fell beside it.

WHEN THE SMOKE CLEARED, the 510 Infantry Battalion was called to formation by its commanding officers. Eighty-two men stood at attention as Colonel Katzenelenbogen approached the troops.

"At ease, gentlemen," the Israeli began. "The battle is over. If any of you fail to realize the outcome, let me explain what would have happened if this attack had been genuine. Live ammunition and fragmentation and concussion grenades would have been used. Instead of cherry bombs at the base of tree trunks, it would have been plastic explosives. In other words, the trees would have come crashing down on you, as well."

Katz paused to let his words sink into everyone's thoughts before he continued. "Between the cross fire of automatic weapons, the exploding grenades and the falling trees, it is unlikely any of you would have survived this encounter," Katz stated. "The United States of America expects the military to be able to provide some protection for national defense. First, you'd better learn how to defend yourselves."

The officers and senior NCOs glared at the Phoenix

Force commander, but they were not in any position to argue with his remarks. They realized Katz was right. The five man assault team would have wiped out the entire battalion.

Christ, *five* men could have killed them all.

"In a combat situation," Katz concluded, "stay alert and ready for action at all times. Next time the dead might not be just a few mannequins. Understand?"

No one argued with this pearl of wisdom.

2

Nothing is more insincere than a diplomatic ball for foreign ambassadors. A convention of clockwork mannequins equipped with tape recordings of monotonously polite dialogue could not be more artificial than the ultraformal dignitaries and bureaucrats who congregate at such social functions.

Admiral Alexander Harker despised such stuffy affairs. A man who still considered himself a sailor at heart, Harker felt dreadfully awkward "dressed as a bloody penguin." Black-tie ceremonies were always a bore. A lot of dull people meeting other dull people and pretending to be thrilled about the whole ruddy business.

Harker shook his head and sighed. He was no stranger to insincerity and deception. In fact, the admiral had spent most of his life in the shadowy world of espionage and intelligence. His career had started during World War II with reconnaissance missions as a young intel officer in the British navy. After the war he was put in charge of all naval intelligence operations in the North Sea region. Harker was then enlisted into Her Majesty's Secret Service.

He became highly suspicious of one of his superiors, a man named George Blake. Harker tried to warn the high-muck-a-mucks of MI6 to keep an eye on Blake, whom he regarded as a probable security risk. His reward was a severe reprimand for his criticism. Blake was one of the most trusted and respected men in the service. Unconvinced that Blake was the sterling chap he appeared to be, Harker persisted. His warnings earned him an obscure observation assignment in the Sudan in 1952, where he would not be an embarrassment at the Home Office.

When MI6 discovered George Blake had in fact betrayed forty British and American agents and given more than a hundred classified documents to the Soviet KGB, a lot of people regretted their dismissal of Harker's warnings. Promoted to the rank of admiral, Harker returned to the United Kingdom where he served as something of a liaison officer for naval intelligence and MI6 until he retired in 1978.

Admiral Harker served as an unofficial adviser even then. Few men could match his background in covert foreign affairs. However, Harker had been invited to the ambassadors' ball at the Banqueting House in recognition of more than forty years of dedication to his country rather than being asked his opinion on clandestine matters.

He had been tempted to stay at home that night and conjure up an excuse for his absence later. But his instincts convinced him to do otherwise. Harker had learned to pay attention to his instincts. They were not infallible, of course. More than once the mental and emotional signals he received turned out to be false alarms. Yet they had been correct more often than not, and they had informed him that he should attend the ball, black-tie nonsense and all.

As the admiral stood in a corner of the ballroom sipping his sherry, he felt the familiar warning signal tap out a message along his spinal cord to his brain. The object of his concern was also the center of attention at the ball.

Ambassador Mafuta was not a sinister figure. A small, slim, black man with distinguished gray hair at his temples and a ready smile, Mafuta did not resemble Patrice Lumumba or Idi Amin. He wore white tie and tails with a multicolored sash draped diagonally across his torso. A bit overformal, perhaps, but a leopard fez or a military uniform with a chest covered with medals would have been cause for concern about the chap. Harker thought Mafuta looked like a decent enough sort, but the signal refused to go away.

Dozens of people shook Mafuta's hand, members of Parliament, bureaucrats from the ministry of foreign affairs and the British ambassador to the United Nations among them. A number of foreign diplomats from various embassies were also present. The Americans, West Germans, French, Japanese and other officials exchanged greetings and professional smiles with Mafuta. Everyone wanted to be friends with the new ambassador.

Mafuta was the official representative sent by the new African nation of Mardaraja, a tiny country somewhere in the Congo region. Mardaraja had not conducted a census, but its population was estimated to be less than a hundred fifty thousand.

Nonetheless, this postage stamp country had attracted international interest. Tai Skrubu, the president of Mardaraja, had announced that his nation would seek to establish relations and trade with the democratic countries of Western Europe, the United States and Japan. Mardaraja seemed especially keen to do business with Great Britain.

A modern African country that requested trade with the United Kingdom was regarded as something of an eighth wonder of the world by Parliament. Britain had lost virtually all influence in Africa—Rhodesia, Ugan-

da and Kenya were no longer British colonies. Great
Britain conducted very little trade with Africa, which
seemed to suit Africa just fine.

However, President Skrubu was on record as stating
that the Soviet Union and Cuban forces in Africa were
the true threat today and Africans should forget past
problems with the British and attempt to make friends
with the United Kingdom. Skrubu publicly denounced
communism and urged treaties with Western powers—
especially England. The British Parliament eagerly
agreed.

Not everyone had been enthusiastic about having the
first Mardarajan embassy in London. The new African
nation had formerly received financial and military
support from Colonel Khaddafi, and the memory of the
Libyan embassy incident still provoked anger and outrage from the British population. How could one trust
any country that was chummy with Khaddafi's regime?

President Skrubu overcame that difficulty by officially severing all ties with Libya and publicly referred
to Khaddafi as a ''terrorist bandit chief.'' The Libyan
strongman replied to this criticism by accusing Skrubu
of ''treason against the forces of liberation throughout
the world'' and ''licking the boots of the imperialistic
West that supports the Zionist gangsters of Israel.''

This mutual character assassination pleased the
British. The majority of critics of Mardaraja were now
willing to accept diplomatic relations with the tiny
African nation. Those who still had doubts were labeled
Victorian snobs and racist reactionaries. They im-
mediately shut up, at least in public.

Admiral Harker had learned that suspicion could be
a virtue. Besides, his instincts still warned him that
something was very wrong about Ambassador Mafuta.
The admiral sensed the same apprehension about the

Mardarajan as he had felt when he first met George Blake.

"I say, Admiral!" Whitney Collins began as he approached Harker. Collins was the minister of state, so Harker could not ignore him, although he would have liked to do so. "So good to see you out and about."

"Thank you, sir," the admiral replied.

"Whatever are you doing over here by yourself?" Collins inquired. "This is a social occasion, you know. Not one of those spy missions you used to be involved with."

"I'd rather you didn't talk about that, sir," Harker told him.

"Come now, Admiral," the minister said, scolding the retired intel officer as one might a child. "This isn't Eastern Europe or the Russian embassy. We're in the Banqueting House, old boy. Look at that ceiling. Magnificent artwork, isn't it? Rubens painted that, you know. King Charles I commissioned him for the job. Ironic that Charles was later executed right outside this very building in. . . ."

"Sixteen forty-nine," Harker said. "Tell me, sir. What do you know about this Mafuta?"

"Seems all right for a colored chap—or whatever Negroes want to be called these days," the minister said, shrugging. "Of course, you know how Africans are. Always looking for a handout of some sort."

"Has anyone talked to him about Khaddafi yet?" Harker inquired.

"Mardaraja isn't doing business with that Arab lunatic anymore."

"So they claim." The admiral nodded. "But I wonder if all the Libyan troops and advisers have pulled out of Mardaraja."

"Intelligence isn't my forte," the minister of state said, shrugging.

"I gathered as much," Harker said dryly. "Is Stanley here by any chance?"

"John Stanley of Security Intelligence Service?" Collins raised his eyebrows. "Good Lord, no. Of course, they sent along a chap for security. You'll find him over in the south wing, I believe. Calls himself Donaldson. Do you imagine that's his real name, Admiral?"

"I imagine it might be," Harker answered. "Thank you, sir. Do enjoy yourself, old man."

The admiral was relieved to get away from Collins and eager to find the SIS operative. Ambassador Mafuta remained the center of attention as Harker hurried across the ballroom. Several UPI reporters were trying to interview the African dignitary, and they thrust microphones at Mafuta like spears as they shoved one another aside in their rush to get close to him.

Flashbulbs popped as cameramen also struggled to get a better position than their peers. The BBC and two American television networks were also covering the event. Their manners were no better than the hyenas from the newspapers.

Admiral Harker quietly slipped through the crowd. No one paid much attention to the portly old man who politely, yet dogmatically slithered past the press representatives. The politicians did not create an obstacle for Harker. They were busy pushing their way in front of the cameras. All of them wanted to be photographed as close to Mafuta as possible.

Politics, Harker thought sourly. The bloody fools would have shaken hands with Jack the Ripper if they thought it would get them some prime time on the telly.

Sadly, public exposure was more popular than patriotism among politicians.

The admiral slipped through the crowd and headed for the south wing. He located Donaldson easily enough. The SIS man was dressed in a gray suit with a walkie-talkie hooked to his belt. Harker approached Donaldson and introduced himself.

"I've 'eard a great deal 'bout you, sir," Donaldson replied, a trace of cockney in his accent. "Pleasure to meet you, sir."

"Thank you," Harker replied. "You don't exactly have a clandestine mission here."

"Bloody politics what it is," Donaldson muttered with disgust. "This bleedin' radio is as obvious as a wart on a stripper's arse, but that's 'ow they want us to 'andle security. No sneakin' 'bout, they say. Let the foreigners see we're 'ere with our bloomin' radios so it'll reassure the silly buggers that they're bein' protected. Damn foolishness, if you ask me, sir."

"What have you been told about Mafuta and the Mardarajan embassy?" Harker asked.

"Not much," Donaldson answered. "Lot of rot 'bout tryin' to make friends with 'em. Seen the Africans movin' into the embassy earlier today. Sent a 'ell of a lot of blokes for such a tiny country in my opinion, sir."

"How many is a lot?" Harker asked.

"Oh, thirty or forty, I reckon," Donaldson said. "Didn't like the looks of some of 'em. Mighty mean lookin' blokes for diplomats, they were. 'Specially the Arabs."

"Arabs?" Harker frowned.

"Diplomats from the Jordanian and Egyptian embassies." Donaldson sighed. "Or that's what they claim anyway. Mardaraja is workin' on gettin' trade with them too."

"Did anyone in SIS check these Arabs?" the admiral asked.

"We were just observers," Donaldson replied. "The blokes from Parliament said we shouldn't 'arass anyone. Said Ambassador Mafuta assured them it was all right."

"And no one checked the luggage and furniture taken into the embassy, either?" Harker urgently inquired.

"We were told not to," Donaldson answered. "Blokes 'ave diplomatic immunity. You know what that means."

"Yes," Admiral Harker said grimly, "I remember exactly what diplomatic immunity can mean."

Neither man paid much attention to a miniature palm tree in an urn at the corner of the hall. If they had inspected it, they probably would not have noticed anything odd about the design of circlets that formed an equator around the base of the urn. The small round emblems disguised a series of wireless microphones that transmitted the conversation to a radio receiver outside the Banqueting House.

Captain Nyoka had heard enough. He removed the earphone and switched off the receiver that sat beside him in the back seat of the gray sedan. Nyoka turned to his companions.

"We have to take care of Admiral Harker," he announced in a casual manner.

Jino smiled, revealing a hideous set of self-mutilated teeth. Following a custom of the infamous Mau Mau terrorists, Jino had filed his lower and upper front teeth until all were pointed to resemble the mouth of a man-eating shark.

A psychotic and a religious fanatic of the primitive faith of the Paka Munga cult, Jino was a sadist who found righteous justification for his cruelty. Murder had been his pastime before it became his profession.

Behind the steering wheel, seated beside Jino, was Patrick McAndrews. A tall, bearded man with a hawk nose and cobalt-blue eyes, McAndrew was a cell leader for the Scottish Liberation Brigade. The SLB was a small terrorist group that was modeled more or less on the image of the Irish Republican Army.

Nyoka and Jino needed McAndrew and his SLB fanatics. The Africans were unfamiliar with London, and they did not have access to contacts within the city or enough vehicles to conduct a proper recon mission. Thus McAndrew's group was necessary. . . for now.

"We didn't think you'd expect us to kill a bloody British admiral," McAndrew said, nervously scratching his reddish-blond beard. "Risky business. Very risky."

"Nothing worthwhile was ever accomplished without risk," Nyoka replied simply. "Contact your comrades, McAndrew. Tell them to get ready."

ADMIRAL HARKER STOOD at the top of the steps of the Banqueting House, thoughtfully puffing a cigar as he waited for his aide to arrive with the car. He didn't have to wait long. The white Mercedes T-300S soon pulled up to the curb.

"How was the party, sir?" Fowler asked as he opened the door for the admiral.

"Stuffy nonsense," Harker replied dryly.

"You have my sympathy, sir," Fowler said sincerely. A former RAF sergeant, Fowler had little use for formal ceremonies full of official snobs and "bleedin' civilians."

The admiral climbed into the back seat. Fowler slid behind the wheel. The sergeant liked the T-300. It was a sport-model Mercedes and the driver's seat reminded Fowler of a cockpit. Driving the admiral's car was a pleasure for the RAF veteran.

Harker crushed his cigar tip in an ashtray as Fowler pulled the Mercedes onto Whitehall. The admiral had decided to contact some friends in the morning. Friends in the SIS and in Parliament. By God, he would find someone to listen.

"Sir," Fowler interrupted the admiral's thoughts. "I do believe we've got somebody following us."

Harker glanced at the rear window. A gray sedan was trailing along behind the Mercedes. The admiral thought it looked like a tail, but he realized that every intelligence operative is a bit paranoid by nature. It is a necessary character trait for survival, like a tightrope walker's sense of balance. Of course, paranoia can also have one jumping at shadows and seeing sinister shapes where none exist.

"Don't do anything rash, Sergeant," Harker advised. "Not until we're sure something's afoot."

Fowler drove past the eighteenth-century religious architecture of St. Martin-in-the-Fields.

The sedan followed Harker's Mercedes onto Charing Cross Road. Fowler turned to the left and pulled onto Shaftesbury Avenue. The sedan was still on their tail.

"I'd say it's official, sir," Fowler remarked as he accelerated to pass a double-decker bus.

"Don't overreact, Sergeant," Harker urged. "But get ready in case it becomes necessary."

"Yes, sir," Fowler agreed as he popped open the glove compartment and removed a Walther P-38 automatic.

The sergeant liked the sturdy German-made pistol; it was built like the turret of a tank. Fowler laid the gun on the seat beside him.

Harker reached under his seat and inserted a slender key into a door hidden by the upholstery. He turned the key and opened the lid. The admiral extracted a compact M-11 Ingram machine pistol from the secret compartment. He slid a long magazine into the butt-well and chambered the first .380-caliber round.

"Which way, sir?" Fowler inquired. "At the moment, we're headed toward the National Gallery."

"Too close to Piccadilly Circus," the admiral said. "Too much traffic in that area. Too many civilians who might be hurt if things get rough."

Fowler turned right on Regent Street. The traffic was not as thick. Only a few vehicles traveled the street that night, Harker noticed with relief.

Suddenly, a lorry burst from an alley. The truck nose-dived into the side of the Mercedes. Fowler tried to fight the wheel, but the car skidded into the next lane and collided with a Citroën. Metal crunched and glass shattered. A woman screamed as the French car was abruptly shoved into the iron fence surrounding a road island.

Two figures rose up at the rear of the lorry, pointed the snouts of Sterling machine guns at the Mercedes and opened fire. Nine-millimeter projectiles pelted the admiral's vehicle. Bullets struck the body and burrowed into the steel skin. Glass cracked and broke. The windshield dissolved.

Sergeant Fowler groaned as three slugs bit into his chest. Incredibly, the tough RAF war horse still managed to raise his Walther and trigger two shots at his assailants.

One of the gunmen dropped his Sterling and slumped from view behind the brackets of the truck. The other Scottish Liberation Brigade killer responded by blasting the Mercedes with another volley of 9mm hail.

Admiral Harker had been thrown to the floor by the impact of the crash. This accident had spared him from the lethal rain of copper-jacketed brimstone. Harker heard the stomach-twisting thump-slush of bullets striking flesh. He felt the backrest of the front seat move as Fowler's corpse jerked from the force of the slugs.

"Bastards," the admiral rasped as he reached for the handle of the car door.

Harker shoved the door open and tumbled outside, the M-11 in his fists. Despite his advanced age and bulky frame, the admiral moved rapidly along the side of the ruined Mercedes. He stayed low, wheezing hard, his heart thundering as if trying to kick a hole in his chest.

The admiral suddenly appeared by the crumpled hood of the T-300S. He thrust the Ingram at the lorry and opened fire. The remaining gunman at the rear of the truck screamed when three .380 rounds ripped into his upper torso and face.

The terrorist fell against the side of the truck, blood gushing from a flap of torn skin that hung from his cheek. The Scot tried to raise his Sterling, but a bullet-shattered shoulder refused to cooperate.

Harker hit him with another 3-round burst. The terrorist's head bounded. Blood and brains spattered from his split forehead. The gunman tumbled over the top bracket and fell to the pavement.

The driver of the lorry aimed an old Webley revolver at Harker and pulled the trigger. The SLB goon was a poor marksman. A .38 slug whined against the frame of the Mercedes. The admiral felt the ricochet slice through the air inches from his face.

Harker was too busy to realize how close he came to death. If the hammering of his heart did not frighten him, neither would a tiny metal hornet that whisked past his face. Harker had already survived two heart attacks in the past and he felt as if he might have a third before the night was over. But not yet. He didn't have time for that sort of thing just yet.

The admiral emptied his Ingram as he sprayed the windshield of the lorry with .380 avengers. Glass burst into a pattern that resembled a road map of Central London. The truck driver slumped behind the wheel, his bloodied head bowed against the horn. The harsh beep raped the air in a continuous, monotonous wail.

Harker stumbled back to the rear of the Mercedes. He leaned against the car as he moved. One hand held the Ingram while the other clutched the left side of his chest, as if holding his heart together.

Then he recognized the dark gray sedan parked behind the wrecked Mercedes. A black man smiled at the admiral with a mouthful of pointy, filed teeth. Harker stared into the muzzle of a Stechkin machine pistol in the terrorist's fists.

"Nguruwe!" Jino hissed. "Pig!"

He squeezed the trigger. Nine-millimeter slugs punched into the admiral's chest and sent him hurtling backward. Harker landed on the pavement. The back of his skull split open when it struck the corner of the curb. The admiral's brains dripped into the rain gutter as his lifeless body trembled slightly from a muscular spasm.

"Oh, God!" Patrick McAndrew gasped, his knuckles white as he gripped the steering wheel of the sedan. "The coppers will be down here quicker than a Limey sailor on his way to a whorehouse."

"You needn't worry about that," Captain Nyoka replied softly as he opened a tan attaché case on his lap.

"What the hell does that—" McAndrew began.

His sentence was terminated along with his life. Patrick McAndrew felt the terrible blazing pain that ripped through his skull like a bolt of satanic lightning. The agony lasted less than a second. McAndrew died too quickly to hear the shot that killed him.

Captain Nyoka had shot the Scottish terrorist in the back of the head. The African returned his Makarov pistol to the briefcase and removed a red canister-style grenade. He closed the valise and opened the car door.

"English police don't carry guns." Jino giggled. "Let's wait for them to arrive. It will be easy to kill some more of the British swine, Captain."

"Don't worry, Jino," Nyoka urged as he stepped from the car. "You'll get to kill some English policemen later. Paka Munga will be very pleased with you before our mission is over. But we've done all the killing we need to do tonight."

Nyoka did not like working with Jino. Religious fanatics are always unstable and Jino worshiped a dark and primitive god that required murder as an act of faith. Such a dangerous zealot could never be trustworthy. Eventually, Jino would have to be destroyed like an attack dog that has become too vicious to be handled, even by its master.

The captain pulled the pin from the grenade and tossed the explosive into the rear of the lorry. The thermite canister exploded, bathing the truck in a white blaze. Pedestrians cried out in terror and fled for shelter. Cars rammed bumpers as drivers slammed on the brakes and bolted away from the flames, fearful the gas tanks would explode at any moment.

Everyone was too busy staying alive to pay much attention to the two Africans who darted into a nearby alley.

The thermite ignited gasoline. The explosion spit fire

and spread the unholy liquid blaze to the Mercedes. Within minutes the admiral's car was a pile of twisted, charred metal.

Six human bodies were transformed into charcoal skeletons. The stench of burning flesh rose from the fire, incense to the gods of destruction and madness.

3

"You guys sure pissed off some of the brass at Fort Jackson," Hal Brognola told the men of Phoenix Force as he methodically chewed a cigar butt, jammed in the corner of his mouth.

"We didn't hurt anybody," Rafael Encizo said with a shrug. "Why should those Army hotshots be angry with us?"

"Because the war games didn't turn out the way they wanted them to," David McCarter answered as he popped the cap from a bottle of Coca-Cola with the blade of his Swiss army knife.

"That's a fact," Calvin James said with a grin. "Aggressors, seven. Army, zero."

Brognola groaned. Since he accepted the duties of the control officer for Stony Man operations, he had learned that the unique character qualities that comprise the personality of an ultimate warrior include a certain lack of respect for authority and contempt for playing by the rules if breaking them will get the job done better.

The Executioner was such a man. When Mack Bolan returned from Vietnam and discovered his family had been victimized by the Mafia, he threw away the rule book and played the game the way he knew best. Bolan declared war on organized crime and fought the mob with all the military skills and weapons' expertise he had acquired in the jungles of Southeast Asia. He was a loner and a renegade, but he brought the Mafia to its knees.

Stony Man had been created to utilize Bolan's deadly talents. The President wanted the Executioner for a war against international terrorism. Bolan was given a new identity as Colonel John Phoenix. To assist in this new war an American foreign legion was formed. The five best antiterrorists in the world were chosen to become the most incredible fighting unit ever assembled. Five men cut from the same warrior cloth as the Executioner himself. The five men of Phoenix Force.

It had been a radical decision to create Stony Man, but the world was in a far more desperate situation than most of its population realized. Terrorism had become more sophisticated and better organized. The sinister hand of the KGB was often behind terrorist activity. The fanatics of these extremist groups were taking suicidal chances that professional espionage agents would not, thus terrorists were carrying out the most dangerous and radical of Moscow's schemes. Worse, sometimes the terrorists took these schemes even further then the KGB had intended.

Many groups that were not associated with the Kremlin were equally dangerous to the safety and freedom of democracy. There were many dragons to be slain, and the combat professionals of Stony Man struck again and again to smash the enemies of peace and civilization.

But Stony Man had also suffered casualties. Andrzej Konzaki, the resident armorer and weapons authority, was killed during an enemy raid on Stony Man headquarters. Aaron "The Bear" Kurtzman had also been a victim. The computer expert was crippled for life and confined to a wheelchair.

The Executioner and Phoenix Force struck back. The terrorists responsible for the raid paid for their treachery, but Bolan's woman, April Rose, was killed in the process.

Then Stony Man faced its greatest challenge of all. The Executioner was forced to leave the organization. Framed for a political assassination by the KGB, Bolan was once again a loner and a renegade. Every police and intelligence network of the free world as well as the Soviet bloc wanted the Executioner—dead or alive.

Stony Man might have been dissolved following the loss of the Executioner, but an insidious plot by a group known as the Black Alchemists required the special talents of Phoenix Force. The five-man army succeeded in defeating the terrorist scheme.

However, Keio Ohara, one of the original members of Phoenix Force, was killed during the final battle at the Black Alchemist stronghold.

Like the warriors who served the organization, Stony Man had endured its ordeals and remained standing, battle-scarred, but unbroken. Tougher than ever.

"A number of the battalion commanders are upset because you five used unorthodox tactics without bothering to warn them about what to expect," Brognola stated, referring to the Fort Jackson war games.

"Unorthodox tactics are part of warfare," Gary Manning commented as he sipped his fourth cup of coffee. "Especially when dealing with guerrillas or terrorists. Washington called the U.S. involvement in Korea and Vietnam 'police actions,' but both were basically guerrilla warfare. I've never heard of a guerrilla outfit that gives advance notice about what kind of tactics it plans to use. They're not known for being sporting in combat."

"Who is?" James remarked dryly.

"Certainly not terrorists," Katz replied. "However, there was ample terrorist activity in Lebanon to warn the Marines that the enemy might use 'unorthodox tactics.' Yet the military wasn't prepared to deal with the truck-bomb version of a kamikaze attack. Washington has to quit sending troops out for 'police actions' and demanding that they behave like security guards for a pipe factory. The armed forces of every free nation *must* learn to cope with terrorism.''

"Well," Brognola sighed. "The main complaint seemed to be that commanding officers objected to the way you chewed everybody's ass after you won the battle. They felt that your criticism was directed against them as well as the enlisted men.''

"Damn right it was," McCarter replied. "The young soldiers have an excuse. They're inexperienced. The leaders have to accept the responsibility. They have to learn to expect the unexpected. If they can't do that, then they shouldn't be leaders—at least, not in a combat situation.''

"Problem is nobody takes war games seriously," Encizo commented. "The military sends troops out on maneuvers, but mock battles are usually preplanned to determine winners and losers. Headquarters has either programmed the mock battles in advance or the odds are stacked to be sure the good guys always win.''

"That's like teaching somebody shadowboxing and expecting him to know how to fight," James commented. "We did those dudes at Jackson a favor, whether they know it or not.''

"Well," Brognola said with a shrug, "you guys sure passed with flying colors.''

"We've functioned successfully as a team in actual combat," Katz stated. "That's more valid than any war games.''

"It wasn't my idea," the Fed reminded Katzenelenbogen. "The President is very concerned about terrorism. He thought the war games would be a way to instruct our military personnel in antiterrorist tactics without jeopardizing the security of Stony Man operations.''

''I'm not so sure it won't jeopardize us,'' Manning declared grimly. ''We used false identification, but literally hundreds of soldiers have a general idea about what Phoenix Force is, even if they don't know us by name. They don't issue halos to guys in the Army. Not all soldiers are patriotic and a lot of them have big mouths. There's no way of estimating how many of those troopers will tell our enemies about us now, either willingly or unwittingly. Maybe the President thinks there was no risk to our security, but I don't agree.''

''Don't get paranoid, Gary,'' McCarter urged cheerfully. ''We'll all feel better when we go into action for real. What's our mission, Hal?''

''Mission?'' Brognola frowned. ''I don't have a mission for you guys yet.''

''What the bloody hell does that mean?'' the Briton snapped. ''Haven't you heard what happened in London a couple nights ago?''

''You're talking about the murder of Admiral Harker,'' the Fed said on a sigh. ''It was definitely a terrorist assassination, but Harker went down fighting. Apparently he took all four assailants with him to the grave. Of course, it's not easy for Scotland Yard to be sure what happened since none of the witnesses got a good look at the gunfight while they were running for cover, and all the physical evidence was badly burned. However, the cops figure one of the terrorists managed to pull the pin from a thermite grenade before Harker shot him. So everybody went up in flames.''

''We heard that much on the radio,'' Encizo commented. ''Hasn't The Bear come up with anything else?''

''Kurtzman gave me an update on the incident just a

couple hours ago," Brognola began as he leafed through a stack of computer printout sheets. "Here it is. Scotland Yard has identified two of the dead terrorists by comparing X rays of their teeth with dental records. The guys were Patrick McAndrew and Angus McCallister. Both were members of the Scottish Liberation Brigade. The SLB is an obscure little group. Probably thought this was a good way to make a name for themselves."

"Harker was an intelligence officer," Katz remarked. "I understand he still acted as an adviser to the SIS and Navy intelligence."

"That's right," Brognola confirmed. "But there's no evidence to suggest Harker was involved in any sort of investigation at the time of his death. Looks like the SLB killed him to settle the score for past actions."

"Doesn't sound like the sort of job Phoenix Force would deal with," Encizo stated.

"The murder of Admiral Harker is a nasty business," Brognola said. "But it doesn't threaten the government of the United States or any of her allies in the free world. I can't send you guys out to deal with every terrorist assassination and act of sabotage that occurs. Hell, terrorism is a daily occurrence. We can't cope with all of it. The Harker incident is closed."

"So we were just supposed to report back to you after the war games were finished?" James asked.

"That's it." Brognola smiled. "Hard to believe, but you guys don't have a mission right now. You've all earned some R and R. Take advantage of it while you can. Maybe we'll be lucky and manage to go a whole month without having to call Phoenix Force to bail out the world."

"Lucky." McCarter snorted with disgust.

4

Ambassador Mafuta nervously puffed a cigarette as he paced the floor of the lobby. He occasionally muttered dark remarks in his native Swahili and shook his head with despair. Jino, the killer with the filed teeth, sat at the foot of a flight of stairs with an AK-47 assault rifle across his knees. He smiled with amusement as he watched the ambassador.

"You're going to wear a hole in that carpet," Jino taunted as he stroked the barrel of his Kalashnikov as one might a woman's thigh.

"This plan is utter madness," Mafuta complained. "I objected to it from the beginning, but no one would listen to me."

"You volunteered," Jino said as he shrugged. "When they told you about the money, you volunteered."

"And you aren't here because of patriotism," Mafuta snapped. "Mardaraja isn't even a real country. It was established solely for this purpose. You're here because you're being paid eighty thousand dinars, so don't preach at me, Jino."

"The money isn't important," the killer declared. "I won't refuse payment, of course, but I would have accepted this mission anyway."

"Don't tell me you believe Khaddafi's propaganda," Mafuta groaned. "The British left Africa two decades ago. The Russians and the Cubans are certainly a greater threat to the independence and freedom of the African people today. Why don't you hate them instead?"

"I do not hate anyone," Jino said, smiling. "But I will kill any person regardless of the color of his skin or his nationality. I worship Paka Munga, so it is my duty to kill. My religious obligation."

Mafuta was startled by Jino's remark. Christian Europeans and Islamic Arabs had all but crushed the old religions of Africa. The worship of nature spirits was labeled "pagan" and "superstitious nonsense." It was evil to bow before false idols, because the Bible and the Koran said so.

The Christians and the Muslims had the written word to support their faith. They also had missionaries and holy men, technology and well-armed soldiers to spread the divine truth. Recently, the Communists had come to Africa with a god named Marx and a saint named Lenin. Yet none of these foreign creeds had been able to totally erase the old religions.

However, few worshiped Paka Munga. Few would want to. Paka Munga is the "cat god," also known as Usika Munga, the god of night. This deity is usually associated with the leopard, which is the most feared and respected of all night creatures. The lion is strong and the cheetah is swift, yet they seldom venture out alone to stalk their prey after dark. The leopard is lord of darkness. He is powerful, fast and fierce—a ruthless loner and the greatest of all night spirits.

The leopard cult was once feared by Africans, who believed tales of supernatural powers that allowed the followers of Paka Munga to transform themselves into leopards. In reality, this black magic was accomplished by the donning of leopard skins complete with claws for weapons. Nonetheless, the evil associated with the leopard-men was all too real—in order to join the cult, an apprentice was required to murder a member of his own family to prove his devotion to Paka Munga.

"I've never really understood your religion," Mafuta confessed.

"Paka Munga is the spirit of the night," Jino explained. "The leopard is his messenger. When I die, Paka Munga will receive me into his fold. I will be a warlord over the souls of those I have killed in this life. By killing, I please Paka Munga. The souls of my victims are held by the night god. I have subjects waiting for me in the next world. Slaves whom I shall command to serve my every need. Do you understand now?"

"I'm beginning to." Mafuta lied because it seemed to be the easiest way of answering the lunatic.

"Of course, you don't," Jino scoffed. "Your ambitions are limited to this world. Even here, you deny yourself the greatest pleasures of the animal that is the most exciting part of being a man. You do not know the thrill of the hunt or the satisfaction of the kill."

"I'm glad you find killing so exciting, Jino," Mafuta snapped. "Will you be so happy about facing your death as well? We'll all be lucky to get out of here alive. . . ."

"Mafuta!" a voice announced sharply. "If you must be a coward, please keep it to yourself. I don't want your spineless attitudes to corrupt the rest of the men."

Mafuta gazed up at the swarthy face that glared down at him from the head of the stairs. A pair of glasses with dark lenses was perched on the bridge of a hawk-bill nose. Thin lips formed a hard line. The man wore a checkered *keffiyeh* headdress, and ammunition belts with Kalashnikov cartridges crisscrossed his khaki shirt.

"I am not a coward, Hizam!" Mafuta shouted at the Arab. "But I'm not a lunatic in love with death either!"

"You shall address me as *Major* Hizam," the Arab said coldly. "And I suggest you prepare for our visitors. Drink some alcohol or take some other sort of drug to tranquilize your fear. If you spoil our plan, I'll be forced to kill you, Mafuta."

"You wouldn't dare," the African replied, but his voice trembled with fear.

"You've been playing ambassador too long, Mafuta," Hizam said, laughing. "That title doesn't mean anything to me. Neither does your life, Mafuta. If you fail to carry out your part of this mission...."

"I'm weary of your threats, Hizam," Mafuta stated, trying to save face to some degree. "I'll do my job. See to it you do likewise."

"I never fail to carry out my duty." Hizam smiled. "No matter what sacrifices it requires."

ASSISTANT SECRETARY EDWARD HEYWOOD wondered if he had made a mistake when he accepted his position with the government of the United Kingdom. His subordinate post with the home secretary's office paid a relatively small salary for a job that was time-consuming and exhausting.

Heywood did not care for most of his duties. He was usually sent to the less desirable functions of the Home Office. His trip to the Mardarajan embassy was such a task. Official opening of the place. Just like a bloody grocery store or a new pub on the block.

"I say," Thornton, the secretary's aide remarked as he gazed out the window of the limousine, "what's all this activity at the embassy about?"

Heywood leaned forward and peered outside. Four or five young black men were marching monotonously in a circle in front of the iron gates surrounding the embassy. They carried cardboard signs bearing legends that claimed President Skrubu was a monster and a butcher of women and children. One poster accused Skrubu of being "the new Idi Amin."

"Student protesters of some sort." Heywood sighed. "Oh, God, I could do without this nonsense. And the Home Office could do without the press coverage this is bound to attract."

"Indeed, sir," Thornton confirmed. "There's a BBC camera crew across the street."

"Lord." Heywood sighed again. "They'll film our arrival. Everyone in the United Kingdom will get to see the disappointment on Ambassador Mafuta's face when he sees I was sent instead of the home secretary."

"He shouldn't be miffed by that," Thornton said. "After all, Mardaraja isn't exactly Saudi Arabia."

"The Mardarajans might be glad of that," Hewyood mused. "No Persian Gulf to worry about. No need to fret about the war between Iraq and Iran...at least no more than the rest of us have to."

"Well, we've got our own little conflict right here to worry about," Thornton commented. "I hope these protesters don't cause a ruddy mess today."

"Don't worry," Hewyood urged, noticing the constables who formed a line beyond the embassy to keep curious bystanders at bay. "We've got protection. I'm certain the police can control a few protesters if things begin to get out of hand."

The chauffeur parked the limo by the curb, and Heywood and Thornton emerged from the car. The protesters backed away from the pair as if they were lepers. The police tensed, fearful of sudden violence.

"Britain must not recognize the Skrubu regime!" a protester cried out. "Do not support a tyrant and murderer!"

However, none of the marchers made an aggressive

move toward the Britons. The doors of the embassy opened and Ambassador Mafuta stepped outside accompanied by Captain Nyoka and another Mardarajan official. All three men wore dark blue pin-stripe suits—the trio were the personification of "civilized Africa."

"Welcome, gentlemen," Mafuta called out in a loud voice. "Welcome to Mardaraja."

"Thank you, Ambassador," Heywood began, trying to conceal his annoyance because Mafuta insisted on communicating from a distance. "If you'll be good enough to open this gate. . . ."

"Of course," Mafuta replied. "It is controlled electronically. I'll have to open it from inside. One moment, please."

Mafuta retreated inside the building. Heywood noticed the protesters began to back away from the fence. Odd, he thought. Perhaps the buggers are concerned about getting too close to Mardarajan property.

"Looks like we'll have a nasty incident after all," Thornton whispered to his employer.

"You worry too much," Heywood replied.

Then his forehead exploded. Blood and brains spit from the exit wound at the back of his skull. Heywood did not hear the report of the shot that killed him. The assistant to the home secretary died on his feet, his corpse wilting to the sidewalk beside his aide.

"My God!" Thornton exclaimed.

A burst of automatic fire erupted from a second-story window. Bullets slammed into Thornton's torso. The impact propelled him backward into the limousine. Thornton's body fell against the hood and slumped lifeless to the pavement.

"Someone call a bleedin' ambulance!" Police Sergeant Willows shouted to his men. "Rest of you lads keep these people away from that damn building."

Willows jogged across the street to the fallen forms of Heywood and Thornton. He realized both men were probably dead, but he had to be certain. Willows was the sort of cop whose conscience would torment him for the rest of his life if he left a person injured on the street without trying to help.

The sergeant did not consider the risk to his own life and limb until another volley of full-auto destruction snarled from the first-story window of the embassy. Willows shrieked as steel-jacketed projectiles struck his legs. Bullets punctured flesh and muscle. Bone splintered and snapped. The sergeant collapsed to the pavement, howling in agony as he clutched his shattered limbs.

The next salvo pelted the crippled officer with murderous slugs. His body tumbled and twitched as blood oozed from a dozen horrible wounds. His fellow policemen, unarmed and unprepared for the crisis, could do nothing but watch Willows die before their eyes.

The driver of the limousine had been stunned by the unexpected mayhem. Paralyzed with fear, he sat frozen behind the wheel and stared at the bullet-shredded corpse of the police sergeant. The chauffeur suddenly recovered from his trance and stomped on the gas pedal.

A front tire rolled over the prone figure of Secretary Heywood. The chauffeur desperately turned the steering wheel to try to avoid running over Sergeant Willows's corpse as well. The limo weaved wildly across the road as a storm of 7.62mm rounds bombarded the car.

Glass burst. The driver screamed as bullets burrowed into flesh and smashed into bone and nerve clusters. The limo plunged down the street and bounced over a curb onto the sidewalk.

The big car nose-dived into a newsstand. The clapboard shed exploded. Magazines and newspapers flew into the air like giant confetti. The limo continued to charge forward until it slammed into the wall of a brownstone apartment building.

Metal crumpled like cardboard. The hood folded into a tent-shaped mutation. A door popped open and the mutilated corpse of the chauffeur tumbled out.

"Bastards!" a constable shouted above the cries of the horrified crowd. "If I had me a rifle, I'd make those slimy burr-heads pay for this!"

"None of that," a sergeant snapped. "Get down the road a bit and help with a blockade. Don't want them picking off motorists who come driving along without suspecting the Mardaraja embassy is full of bloody killers."

"Lord help us all," a BBC reporter rasped, staring at the bloodied corpses that littered the street. "This is a nightmare."

"Nightmare, is it?" the sergeant inquired. "Well, those blokes out there aren't going to wake up, mate. If this is a nightmare, it isn't the kind that ends so easy."

Perhaps, he thought, it will never truly end. . . .

5

Major Abdul Hizam watched the activity in the London streets below. He smiled with satisfaction. His stomach was warm as if he had just eaten a mutton dinner and washed it down with hot coffee. The Arab felt the barrel of his Kalashnikov. It too was warm. Hot, like Hizam's passion for his work.

Unlike Jino, Major Hizam's satisfaction was not based on a belief in Paka Munga or a spiritual reward in the next life. Hizam considered himself to be a devout Muslim and a patriotic Libyan, but his true faith was not in Allah, but in Colonel Moammar Khaddafi.

Hizam was a nationalistic Libyan and a Khaddafi loyalist. He had received his field grade promotion from Khaddafi personally. For Hizam this was the ultimate honor and it ensured his absolute dedication to the strong man of Libya.

To most people, Hizam realized, Colonel Khaddafi was nothing more than a madman, an oil-rich lunatic who used his wealth to finance international terrorism. But Khaddafi was a very popular leader among his people in Libya.

Since Khaddafi's successful coup in 1969, when the colonel's regime replaced the Libyan monarchy, the standard of living in Libya had improved dramatically. Khaddafi's radical policies against Israel and the powers of the West that support the Jewish state, didn't disturb Hizam and his fellow Libyans. The people of

Libya considered the Zionists and their allies to be the real terrorists.

Khaddafi had also done considerable business with the Soviet Union, buying billions of dollars' worth of Russian weaponry and financing KGB-related terrorism in Western Europe and the Middle East. Yet he had been careful not to form too close a partnership with the Soviets.

Hizam considered Khaddafi to be the soul of Libya. It was the major's patriotic duty to serve his leader. Allah had sent Khaddafi to rule Libya. Thus, Hizam reasoned, he also had an obligation to God to follow the colonel's orders without question. The major was a total fanatic, emotionally and spiritually convinced that his cause was not only justified but righteous, as well.

"The second phase of our mission is a success," Hizam announced proudly, turning from the window. "Allah is with us, my brothers."

"Indeed," Lieutenant Khaled, his second-in-command, agreed. "The will of God shall be done and the infidel devils of this accursed country shall suffer for their sins against our divine leader."

Captain Nyoka concealed his contempt for the Libyans. A mercenary and an atheist, Nyoka considered politics and religion to be utter nonsense—unless he could make a profit via one or the other. Nyoka thought the Libyans were pea-brained morons who had fallen in love with Colonel Khaddafi, the leader of a third-rate power who was pushing the big boys of the West harder than any rational man would dare.

Nyoka had learned the fundamentals of intelligence and espionage in the 1960s when the CIA organized counterguerrilla forces in the Congo. Already a cold-blooded killer, Nyoka gave lip service to all the proper anti-Communist jargon as the American agents instructed him in reconnaissance, surveillance and the more sophisticated methods of assassination.

The young African was an eager student and learned his trade well. After the early conflicts in the Congo ceased, Nyoka sold his deadly skills to anyone willing to pay enough to suit him. He joined Idi Amin's secret police until the Israelis hit the Entebbe airport to rescue a planeload of hostages in 1976. Amin was making some powerful enemies, and his days in Uganda were numbered. Nyoka decided it was time to move on.

He later served as a mercenary in Angola, where he fought for both sides, changing allegiance when it seemed clear the Communists would be victorious. In 1978 Nyoka joined the Patriotic Front led by Joshua Nkomo and participated in the guerrilla war in Rhodesia.

Eventually, he found himself back in the Congo just in time to be part of the new republic of Mardaraja. Once again, he found a market for his lethal talents. Nyoka did not like Khaddafi, but he did not care if the Libyan strongman was the man behind the scheme. For eighty thousand dinars, Nyoka would have worked for Satan himself. Some people said he already did.

"How long will we have to wait here?" Nyoka asked as he leaned against the doorway and watched the Libyans reload their Kalashnikov autorifles.

"That will depend on the British," Hizam replied simply. "Probably less than a week."

"I hope you're right, Major." Nyoka sighed. "We've got a limited supply of food and bottled water. I doubt that it'll last more than a week. We've got too many people in this embassy and we're going to feel more crowded than sardines in a can before this is over. If the British decide to starve us out...."

"They won't." Hizam smiled. "It wouldn't be civilized, don't you know. The British follow certain rules of conduct in this sort of situation. They'll probably start sending us packages of food and cigarettes by tomorrow evening. Part of keeping the lines of communication open. The British believe in that."

"That's how the English behaved when your comrades first played this stunt at the Libyan embassy last year," Ambassador Mafuta declared. "I certainly hope they haven't decided to resort to the same tactics they used at the Iranian embassy instead. In case you don't remember, they sent in the SAS, who raided the building and—"

"The British won't raid this embassy for the same reason they didn't lay siege to the Libyan embassy," Hizam explained. "To do so would be an act of war. This building is officially Mardarajan territory according to international law. The British would not dare touch us as long as your country has diplomatic relations with Britain."

"You're not certain of that, Major," Mafuta sneered. "And neither is your little tin god, Colonel Khaddafi. If he didn't suspect the English might try to attack the embassy, why did he insist we bring so many men for this mission? Why do we have so many weapons? Only five or six are needed to carry out the...."

Hizam suddenly aimed his AK-47 at the ambassador. The Libyan worked the bolt of his weapon to chamber the first cartridge. Mafuta's mouth fell open and his eyes expanded in terror. Hizam smiled coldly at the display of fear on the African's face.

"We really don't need you anymore, Mafuta," Hizam warned. "I could kill you right now and still complete our mission."

"Wait a minute, Major," Nyoka urged. "Like you

said before, the British will want to keep a line of communication open with the embassy. If the ambassador doesn't reply, they might just get upset enough to get nasty. Personally, I don't want to get boxed into this place while all the SAS and Royal Marines in England are lobbing grenades and mortar shells through the windows."

"All right," Hizam said as he lowered his rifle, "you get to live for a while, Mafuta. Just keep your mouth shut and you might even get to leave here alive."

"I wonder if any of us will leave here alive," Mafuta muttered sourly.

"Perhaps not," Hizam said with a shrug. "But whether we survive or not, a great many British will die before this affair is over."

6

David McCarter stood at the threshold of the Neville Academy of Butler and Valet Instruction. A young man dressed in a dark suit and vest opened the door for the commando.

"Hello, Mr. McCarter," the youth greeted formally, unruffled by the shabby appearance of the Phoenix Force pro. McCarter was dressed in a ragged sweatshirt, soiled jeans and sneakers. "I believe you are expected, sir."

"I am unless they decided to have somebody else teach the bloody class today," McCarter replied gruffly.

He entered a plush hallway with an ornate stairwell and reproductions of famous paintings on the walls. McCarter strolled into the next room and viewed a parlor with Victorian furniture and a great fireplace complete with an Excalibur-type sword above the mantle.

A group of trainees, studying to become proper English butlers, were walking around in a circle with wineglasses perched on their heads. Jennings, a veteran butler turned instructor, kept telling the lads to look straight ahead and watch their posture. Occasionally a glass fell and shattered on the floor. No one paid much attention to this. Jennings simply put another glass on the trainee's head and told him to try again.

"Good afternoon, Mr. McCarter," Jennings said when he noticed the commando. "I believe your students are waiting for you, sir."

"They'd better be," McCarter replied. "Nobody is allowed to be late to one of my classes except me."

He moved to a den. A crystal chandelier hung from the ceiling. Trainees dressed in black suit and tie were practicing pouring champagne and carrying the glasses on silver trays. McCarter slipped past them and moved to a corridor.

If anyone had told David McCarter that one day he would be instructing a group of aspiring butlers and valets, he would have told that individual to get lost. Yet, here he was in the Neville Academy about to do just that.

The only problem with being a member of Phoenix Force, in McCarter's opinion, was the fact he did not receive a regular salary and had to maintain some sort of job for the sake of appearances. This was easier for his teammates. Katz and Encizo were officially self-employed. Manning was the senior vice-president of North America International and he could pretty much come and go as he pleased. Calvin James had enrolled in the Arlington College of Surgery in Virginia. A government grant, arranged by Hal Brognola, was paying for James's education and most of his bills.

McCarter, however, had difficulty keeping a job because his main passion in life had always been his love for adventure and excitement. His only talents were paramilitary. McCarter had worked as a flying instructor and a test driver for automobiles, but his short temper and sharp tongue cost him both jobs.

Yet McCarter was not really a bad sort. He simply became frustrated and surly with the monotony and safety of civilian occupations. McCarter was a man of war. His entire life since childhood had been dedicated to acquiring the abilities that made him a superb commando and fighting man. Unfortunately, this failed to prepare him for making a living in a society that was more or less at peace.

McCarter located the gymnasium and opened the door. His class had already assembled inside. The would-be butlers were dressed in white judo *gi* uniforms with different color belts to determine their martial-arts rank. Most wore the white belts of beginners, but a few sported the green belts of advanced students and two had been awarded brown belts by their *sensei* instructors.

The chaps with the green and brown belts had received their higher ranks while taking courses in *goju-ryu* karate at a local *dojo*. They had asked McCarter what rank he held, obviously expecting him to have a black belt, second or third *dan* at least. They were disappointed when McCarter admitted that he had never been awarded a belt of any color except "the one issued with my uniform when I was in the bloody army."

"What the hell do they think they're doing?" McCarter growled when he noticed two of the students punching and kicking each other.

"Walker and Sommers had a bit of a tiff, sir," a trainee explained. "Sommers was quite a boxer in college and he reckons boxing is better than karate. Walker, being a second *dan* brown belt, got a bit upset with that. One thing led to another and they decided to settle the matter physically."

"Bloody idiots," McCarter muttered.

Sommers, the boxer, had stripped off his belt and *gi* jacket. Sweat shimmered on his well-muscled upper torso as he danced and weaved in front of his opponent. His fists were held in front of his face, ready to guard or attack if necessary.

Walker adopted a T-*dachi* stance. He held one arm

extended and the other close to his hip. Both men had already scored a few blows, their faces marred by bruises. Walker attacked, launching a karate kick at Sommers's groin.

The boxer dodged the kick and ducked under a slashing *shuto* chop aimed at his head. Sommers hooked a punch to Walker's ribs and rammed an uppercut to his opponent's midsection. Walker staggered and Sommers swung a solid left to Walker's face.

Walker's head bounced from the punch and he swayed on unsteady feet. Sommers hit him with a left jab to the chin and swung a right cross. Walker's left forearm blocked the attack. The heel of his right palm struck the boxer under the jaw.

Sommers stumbled. Walker's *kiai* shout filled the room as he pumped a *seiken* ram's-head punch to his opponent's breastbone. Sommers groaned and fell back into a wall. Walker's right leg unleashed a high side kick. His bare foot slammed into Sommers's face. The boxer fell to the mat-covered floor.

Walker stepped back and waited for Sommers to get up. The boxer rose and both men squared off. McCarter decided it was time to break up the fight. Without warning, he moved behind Walker and shoved the karate man into Sommers. Both combatants fell against the wall.

"You blokes want to fight?" McCarter inquired. "Try me."

Walker whirled and swung a crescent kick at McCarter's head. The commando weaved out of the path of his feet. Walker launched a *seiken* punch. McCarter parried the attack with a palm and hooked a fist to the karate man's face. Before Walker could recover and counterattack, the Phoenix Force fighter quickly swept a foot to the back of Walker's ankle and tripped his opponent.

Walker went down, but Sommers moved in swiftly and swung a fist at McCarter's face. The commando's arm blocked the attacking limb and his hand snared the boxer's wrist. McCarter's left hand chopped Sommers's other arm before the boxer could throw another punch.

McCarter whipped a knee into his opponent's abdomen and quickly butted his forehead into Sommers's face. The boxer's head recoiled from the unexpected blow. McCarter seized Sommers, turned slightly and hurled the boxer over his hip. Sommers hit the floor hard. McCarter stomped a foot on the mat next to his adversary's ear.

Walker had gotten to his feet. The karate man snarled a furious *kiai* as he leaped into the air and executed a flying jump kick. Walker rocketed toward McCarter, right leg extended, bare foot aimed at the commando's head.

McCarter deftly sidestepped, and a surprised Walker sailed harmlessly past the Phoenix Force pro. McCarter lashed a forearm into the karate man's lower back. Walker convulsed in midair and fell awkwardly to the mat. He rolled and started to rise. McCarter stepped forward and kicked him in the ribs.

"I say," a trainee spectator remarked, "not very sporting."

"Bad form," another agreed.

Walker rolled away from McCarter and desperately scrambled to his feet. Enraged, the karate man charged forward and launched a high roundhouse kick at the commando's head. McCarter easily dodged the kick and grabbed Walker's ankle in both hands.

McCarter's foot shot out. Walker groaned with pain when the kick struck the muscle of his inner thigh. The commando twisted the man's ankle forcibly and threw Walker off balance. The karate man tumbled across the mat once more.

Sommers had gotten up again. McCarter turned to face him, but the boxer held his hands up in surrender. Walker rose slowly, rubbing his bruised thigh muscle with both hands.

"I've had enough too, sir," he announced. "I hope you'll accept my apology."

"I could have kicked your balls in, mate," McCarter snapped. He turned to Sommers. "Or stomped your silly face."

"I know, sir," the boxer replied sheepishly.

"Bloody awful behavior for a couple blokes that plan to be gentlemen's gentlemen." McCarter shook his head in despair. "Brawling like a pair of kids from the East End. That's the sort of thing you'd expect from an uncouth lout like me."

McCarter folded his hands at the small of his back as he moved to the center of the room. The students shuffled out of his way. The commando turned to face them.

"I was hired to teach you chaps how to take care of yourselves and protect your future employers," McCarter began. "These days, folks expect a butler to defend them from kidnappers, terrorists and other types of lowlife. That means I have a job to do and I won't tolerate any of you wasting my time. I don't want you brawling like spoiled brats at a boys's school."

McCarter shrugged. "Well, maybe you blokes can learn something from today's experience. First, Walker and Sommers were fighting according to the rules of their particular styles. There's no referee in a real fight. No Queensberry rules, no judge to give you points for fancy high kicks. Survival is the only reward.

"Don't get too fond of any style," McCarter continued. "Karate, boxing, kung fu, street-fighting tactics, all have strengths and weaknesses. If a technique works, *it works*. That's what matters...."

The door opened. Jennings, the senior butler, appeared at the threshold. He announced that Mr. McCarter had a visitor waiting for him in the parlor.

"Male or female?" McCarter inquired.

"A gentleman, sir," Jennings replied.

"I'll see who it is anyway," McCarter declared. "You blokes work on fundamentals for a while. Stance, breaking your fall and all that rot until I get back. You can also think about the second thing you should have learned today. Don't get me pissed off."

THE PHOENIX FORCE PRO was surprised to discover who his visitor was. Major Hillerman was waiting for him in the parlor. Hillerman had been McCarter's commanding officer during the SAS involvement in the Omani Ohofar War.

Odd how most people forget about the "little wars," McCarter thought. Most do not remember that the British military was stationed in Oman between 1970 and 1976. But the Special Air Service remembered. Twelve commandos of the elite fighting unit died in Oman. Twelve more names were added to the list of the dead at the base of the clock at the SAS headquarters at Hereford.

The Omani Ohofar War was a nasty little conflict that consisted of fighting Communist guerrillas trained and armed in Marxist South Yemen. Most of the action was in the mountainous region by the border. The fighting was sporadic, but savage. The worst part had been waiting for the guerrillas to make their move.

No, McCarter thought. The worst part had been sitting up all night with an SAS corporal who was dying from a stomach wound. Or the day Captain Hillerman's right leg was ripped to pieces by shrapnel. They had to amputate at the knee. McCarter would never forget the sound of the bone saw ripping through Hillerman's joint, or the scream of agony when the morphine wore off before the medics completed the operation.

After the Omani Ohofar War, McCarter remained in the SAS. He served in a covert police action in Hong Kong and participated in Operation Nimrod, the successful siege of the Iranian embassy in London in 1980. Hillerman was transferred to Special Military Intelligence and given a desk job and a field-grade promotion.

The two men always stayed in touch. Since McCarter joined Phoenix Force, Hillerman had been an ally McCarter could trust without reservations. Although the major did not know about Phoenix Force, he was aware McCarter was involved in a top-secret international commando operation of some sort. Hillerman often helped McCarter transport arms and equipment out of the United Kingdom. He helped supply forged documents and cut through red tape when necessary. But most importantly he trusted McCarter enough not to ask questions.

"Hello, Sergeant," Hillerman greeted as he limped forward, assisted by a walnut walking stick. "Never expected to find you in a place like this."

"I work here," McCarter replied.

"Teaching jujitsu to student butlers?" the major inquired.

"Something like that," McCarter said. "I'm also teaching the lads combat pistol shooting on the weekends. Most of them will probably wind up working for some rich Yank in the States. Since America is full of cowboys and gangsters, an English butler ought to learn to handle a gun, eh?"

"Can we talk privately, Sergeant?" Hillerman asked.

"Sure," McCarter said, nodding. "Follow me, sir."

He led Hillerman to a side door and they entered an indoor garage. A black Bentley and a sky-blue Jaguar were parked inside. Hillerman took out a cigarette case, opened it and offered a smoke to McCarter.

"Thank you, major," the commando said, accepting a cigarette. "What's on your mind, sir?"

"I've often wondered what sort of group you're connected with these days," Hillerman began as he fired his lighter and held the flame for McCarter. "Every now and then I come across a bit of unconfirmed intelligence data that mentions five professional commandos. No one seems quite sure what they are—mercenaries, antiterrorists, foreign agents. However, they're obviously on our side and they always manage to get the job done. Oddly enough, none of these reports ever seem to get confirmed. In fact, most of them disappear from our files."

"Please don't get too curious, Major," McCarter urged, puffing his cigarette gently. "I don't want to have to lie to you."

"One thing I've learned in intelligence," Hillerman said, smiling, "is no one ever knows all the facts about anything. Most of us work in the dark so often we feel like ruddy bats most of the time. I don't need to know any details about your operation, Sergeant. I only want to ask for a favor."

"I owe you more than one, sir," McCarter said. "But I can't promise I'll be able to oblige you."

"I realize that," the major replied as he leaned against the Bentley and propped his artificial leg along the running board. "And I know if you can help, you will. You've got your share of flaws, Sergeant—"

"As many as I can get away with," McCarter interrupted.

"But a lack of patriotism has never been one of them," Hillerman continued. "A situation occurred less than an hour ago that concerns national security and domestic safety for our people. To say nothing of England's national honor and pride."

"Oh, God!" McCarter rolled his eyes. "What's Prince Andrew done now?"

"This is serious, Sergeant," Hillerman snapped. "Four British subjects were murdered in broad daylight by terrorist gunmen inside the Mardaraja embassy."

McCarter did not joke as he listened to the details of the incident. His face tensed with anger. Like most red-blooded Englishmen, McCarter had been outraged by the Libyan embassy incident in 1984. A sniper inside the embassy had opened fire on a group of protesters. A policewoman working crowd control was killed by the gunman.

The world watched as British police and military surrounded the Libyan embassy. Days passed. The vigil continued. SAS commandos were stationed on rooftops, eagerly waiting for permission to raid the building. Perhaps if the Libyans had fired another shot, Britain would have struck back. But the snipers in the embassy did not act again, and the waiting continued.

Colonel Khaddafi made some ridiculous claims that the British had arranged the entire incident just to discredit his regime. The colonel never explained why London would have authorized the murder of a policewoman instead of having a few Libyan protesters shot instead. Naturally, Khaddafi refused to order the Libyans inside the embassy to surrender or grant permission for the British to storm the building.

At last, Great Britain severed diplomatic relations with Libya. Frustrated and furious, the British people watched helplessly as the occupants of the embassy were given safe passage back to their homeland. The murderer or murderers went scot-free and unpunished.

The Libyan ordeal had left a painful scar on the national pride of the United Kingdom. It was a bitter taste in the mouth of the British lion. Now, the nightmare was about to happen again.

"Parliament can't authorize a raid on the embassy," Hillerman concluded. "That would be considered an act of war by Great Britain upon the republic of Mardaraja."

"Piss on the republic of Mardaraja," McCarter gritted. "How many times does this sort of thing have to happen before Parliament learns it can't play bloody games with terrorists?"

"It's a matter of international law," the major explained. "Parliament can't change the rules until the rest of the world agrees to do likewise. But we can't allow this to happen again. We can't let those Mardarajan killers just sit in their embassy and wait for diplomatic relations to be severed so they can return to Africa and brag about how they got away with murder in England. We have to show the whole bloody world that Great Britain is not powerless against this sort of terrorism."

"Since the police and the SAS can't do it," McCarter began, "you're suggesting I contact some friends and we launch our own raid on the embassy, right?"

"I'm a government official now, David," Hillerman replied with a shrug. "I can't advise you about something like that. Why, that would virtually be a criminal act against a foreign embassy. Of course, the British government wouldn't be at fault if a group of foreign mercenaries of some sort attacked the Mardarajan embassy."

"Sounds delightful," McCarter agreed. "But the

police and the SAS will have the place surrounded. They can't just look the other way while we attack the building. Any idea how we can get past those lads in order to carry out the assault?''

"Haven't the foggiest, Sergeant," Hillerman confessed. "But you were always a resourceful fellow. I'm certain you'll come up with something."

7

"Mr. Torberg?" McCarter spoke into the mouthpiece of a radio transceiver that transmitted via a communications satellite to a similar transceiver located in Peerview, Vermont.

"This is Torberg," Colonel Yakov Katzenelenbogen replied. "I rather expected you to call Mr. Carver."

"Really?" The Briton smiled. Katz had obviously heard about the Mardaraja embassy—it was a feature news story throughout the world by the time McCarter contacted the Phoenix Force commander. "I was wondering if you've decided whether or not to take your vacation in England this year?"

"I'm all for it," Katz confirmed, well aware of what McCarter was really talking about. "Of course, I'll have to see if everyone else agrees."

"Are you going to ask your employer for time off?" the Briton inquired, actually asking if Katz intended to contact Brognola about the mission.

"I'm sort of on vacation right now," Katz answered. "Between assignments, you might say. No reason to contact the office until later. To do so now would just get the old man's blood pressure up."

"I don't want you to feel you have to rush out here," McCarter urged. "Wouldn't want you to put your job on the line, mate."

"Don't worry about that," the Israeli replied. "I think I can get away for a few days. The rest of the family may not be able to make the trip, but I think they'll be delighted to drop whatever they're doing and join me if they can. No promises, you understand.''

"I understand," McCarter assured him. "About when can I expect you?"

"Probably next week," Katz stated. "Thursday or Friday, unless we can get an earlier flight."

McCarter knew "next week" meant "tomorrow." "Thursday or Friday" translated as late evening or perhaps the following morning.

"Of course," Katz added, "we'll have trouble getting accommodations set up in advance. Can you help with that?"

"I've already started taking care of that," McCarter replied.

"Very good," Katz said. "Unless there are some unforeseen complications, we'll get together next week."

"I'm very glad to hear that, Mr. Torberg," McCarter said sincerely. "Thank you."

"Thank you, Mr. Carver." Katz chuckled. "Believe me, I'm looking forward to the trip."

"I just hope everything goes smoothly when you get here," the Briton confessed. "We might have a problem or two."

"We'll talk about that later," Katz declared. "Take care, Mr. Carver."

"You do the same, Mr. Torberg," McCarter replied.

DAVID MCCARTER DROVE his BMW into the carport of the Kensington Apartments on High Street, only a couple blocks from Kensington Palace. The luxury car had been one of McCarter's benefits when he had been a test driver. The BMW was sold to him at a ridiculously low price, which turned out to be compensation for equally ridiculously low wages.

McCarter parked the BMW and headed for his flat. The apartment revealed his paramilitary personality. The furniture was brown leather, the carpet artillery red. Most of the books on the shelves were training manuals dealing with strategy, weapons, hand-to-hand combat and survival in various hostile environments. There was also a great number of books about military history. A few were written in French, which McCarter kept basically to maintain his ability in that language. Like most Englishmen, he found little in the French version of history that he agreed with.

McCarter also had several biographies of historical heroes in his library. Most were British and all were a bit eccentric with a maverick streak in their character. Sir Francis Drake, General Charles Gordon, Sir Winston Churchill and Colonel "Mad Mike" Horce were among his favorites.

The flat was clean and neat, the carpet recently vacuumed and the furniture wiped of dust. This was contrary to McCarter's nature. Neatness was just one quality of the military that had failed to rub off on McCarter. However, he now had help with his housekeeping.

"About time you got back," Janis Perry complained as McCarter entered the apartment.

"My God," he muttered. "You're learning how to nag. So much for the perfect woman in my life."

"If I was perfect," she replied with a good-natured grin, "we'd have nothing in common."

It was good to see her smile. When McCarter first met Janis, she had forgotten how to smile. Twenty-nine years old, Janis was a junior executive for an advertising firm. She was bright and clever with a good sense of humor. She had a nice figure, long legs and silky brown hair.

But Janis had been the victim of a car accident. The right side of her face was marred by a spiderweb of scar tissue. One eye was milky white and blind. Yet the worst scars had been mental and emotional.

Abandoned by her former fiancé and treated with insincere prattle by a psychologist who could barely stand to look at her, Janis tried to hide from the world. She feared contact with men, certain she would always be regarded as a disfigured freak. Until she met David McCarter.

"Sorry I'm late, luv," McCarter said as he closed the door. "Something unexpected came up."

"Not another secret mission that you can't talk about?" Janis groaned.

"Afraid it looks that way," he confessed.

"Then you'll be leaving soon." Janis sighed. "Running off to God-knows-where to do God-knows-what."

"I warned you about this, luv," McCarter told her, placing his hands on her shoulders. "All I can tell you is my work is important."

"I know that whatever you do," she whispered, "you always take a gun with you."

"Tools of the trade."

"You have a license to kill?" she asked dryly.

"I'm working on it," he joked. "Right now I've just got a learner's permit on advanced mayhem."

"I worry about you," Janis said softly. "I don't know that I could bear losing you."

"Don't expect too much from me," he warned, gazing at her scarred features. McCarter had learned to love that face and he found her genuinely beautiful. "I can't promise you anything."

"You've given me a lot already, David," Janis replied. "I'd probably still be hiding in the shadows, feeling sorry for myself if I hadn't met you."

"Some other chap would have come along." McCarter shrugged. "Probably not as dashing and charming as I am, of course."

"Or as modest," she said, laughing.

"That too," he agreed. "Seriously, luv, I worry about you too."

"No need to," Janis assured him. "I can look in the mirror now without flinching. After all, how could I doubt that you find me attractive? You're such a bloody great animal in bed."

"That's not what I mean," McCarter explained. "I'm talking about a possible threat to life and limb."

"I know," she said. "Whatever your business is, it's dangerous and some of that danger might splash over on me. I don't care about that, David."

"I do," he told her. "You know this relationship isn't going to last forever."

"No relationship ever does," Janis replied. "Plan to give me the boot, luv?"

"No," McCarter answered. "I probably should, but I'm a bit too selfish."

"I forgive you," Janis said as she wrapped her arms around his neck.

Their lips brushed, and their tongues probed the familiar caverns of each other's mouths. Hands caressed gently, moving faster as passion increased.

"Well," Janis said in a husky whisper, "if you'll be leaving soon, let's not waste any time tonight."

8

The following morning, McCarter drove to the site of the Mardarajan embassy. The area was blocked off by the police. Traffic was rerouted by constables who had their hands full keeping the curious at bay. McCarter pulled his BMW up to the blockade, and a constable immediately appeared at his window.

"You'll have to move on, sir," the officer told him. "Can't have civilians hanging about with all this trouble at the embassy and such."

"I'm not exactly a civilian," McCarter replied as he showed the constable a military ID card. "I'm with the reserves, SAS, although I'm not on active duty at this time."

"Still doesn't authorize you in this area, sir," the constable insisted.

"Not trying to cause anyone any problems, officer," McCarter assured him. "But I might be able to help. I was part of the SAS raid on the Iranian embassy in 1980."

"Operation Nimrod?" The officer raised his eyebrows. "Lord, I'd dearly love to see you chaps handle this mess the way you handled that Iranian business."

"Maybe your wish will come true," McCarter replied. "Let me talk to whoever's in charge here."

"I'll take you to my sergeant," the constable replied. "Perhaps he can help you, sir."

McCarter had to go through the chain of command.

He tolerated the delay as best he could. Patience had never been one of his virtues, but McCarter kept his temper as he was escorted from sergeant to inspector and finally to Police Lieutenant Haleron.

Haleron was basically concerned with crowd control and traffic. He had a mobile headquarters in the back of a lorry that included a field radio and an assortment of firearms, tear-gas grenades and riot gear. Although British police do not generally carry guns, most are trained in the use of firearms in case an emergency requires more than a truncheon for weaponry.

"Well, Mr. McCarter," Haleron began wearily, "I've told my radio operator to contact the SAS stationed at the area immediately surrounding the embassy. If their commanding officer agrees to meet with you, we'll send you in. Sound fair enough?"

"Can't ask for more than that," McCarter replied.

"Lieutenant," the radio operator announced as he pulled off his headset, "I just spoke with a gent with the SAS. Their officer in charge seems to know Mr. McCarter. He recognized the name immediately and authorized Mr. McCarter to come ahead, sir."

"Bloody good." McCarter sighed with relief.

Haleron insisted that McCarter wear a flak vest and riot helmet, and although the commando didn't like such clumsy gear, he agreed to this request. A constable, also clad in riot gear and armed with a Winchester shotgun, accompanied the Phoenix Force pro.

The streets were quiet, but far from deserted. Newspaper and television reporters were positioned inside the restricted area, although they were not permitted within six hundred yards of the embassy. TV cameras followed McCarter and the constable, but the reporters didn't ask any questions—which suited McCarter just fine. He was glad the riot helmet visor concealed his face.

Two armored cars were parked across the street from the embassy. The vehicles provided cover for half a dozen men dressed in the khaki uniform and sand-colored berets of the Special Air Service. McCarter smiled. It was always good to see his old regiment again.

Of course, he didn't recognize the faces. Most of the fellows who had been in the SAS with McCarter had been replaced by younger men. Thirty is middle-aged in the military. Forty is an old man. McCarter was almost thirty-five, but he didn't worry about becoming an old man. That was not likely to happen to anyone in Phoenix Force.

McCarter glanced at the Mardarajan embassy. The building was three stories high, with a garret beneath the lead-tiled roof. Two men were stationed on the roof. They wore heavy tweed jackets that suggested they were accustomed to the chilly autumn weather in England. Neither man held a visible weapon, but both carried binoculars.

The building was made of brick and mortar. Most of the windows were wide, with thick curtains that concealed activity within. Yet more than one set of drapes had been drawn back. Faces peered out, watching everyone and everything.

McCarter walked toward the armored cars, knowing full well that a sniper with a good rifle and an accurate scope could easily pick him off. Riot helmets will not stop a high-velocity bullet, and an armor-piercing projectile can punch through a flak vest as if it were cardboard. In the SAS they speak about "beating the clock," referring to the great clock at Hereford that bears a list of the dead. No one can beat the clock forever, and McCarter was not frightened by the fact his time would probably run out sooner than most.

"Hurry up," an SAS sergeant snapped. "Get your

arse over here before those blighters decide to shoot it off!''

"If they wanted to kill us," McCarter replied, his voice distorted by the helmet, "they would have done it already, mate.''

The sergeant jammed his fists in his hips and glared at McCarter. He was a big man with a handlebar mustache, stiff with hair wax. The NCO had more hair on his upper lip than his head. The tan beret covered the top of his dome, but the sides appeared to be shaved. "Hutton" was printed on the name tag above his breast pocket.

"You must be McCarter," Hutton snorted. "The major said you always were a bloody know-it-all with a big mouth.''

"The major?" McCarter groaned. "That couldn't be Major Simms by any awful chance?''

"Not by chance at all, McCarter," a voice announced.

McCarter had hoped he would never hear that voice again, but fate has a habit of dashing our fondest dreams to bits. Major Geoffrey Simms emerged from a coffee shop, big as life and twice as pompous.

Simms was a tall, wiry man. Six foot three and about a hundred and seventy pounds. His face was long with pinched cheeks, a ski-slope nose and bushy gray-brown eyebrows mounted above pale green orbs.

"Well, fancy meeting you here," McCarter muttered as he slipped off his helmet.

"You look better with that bucket over your head," Simms sneered. "If you want to talk to me, get your arse inside that coffee shop. *Now!*''

McCarter bit his tongue before he could make a hasty, rude remark. Reluctantly he entered the shop. Simms and Sergeant Hutton followed him inside.

"Face the wall, McCarter!" Simms snapped. "Spread-eagle!"

"What the bloody—" McCarter began.

"You heard the major," Hutton growled as he suddenly thrust a palm between McCarter's shoulder blades. "Do it or I'll bust your bleedin' head, lad!"

The shove sent McCarter staggering into a wall. Furious, the hot-tempered commando whirled to face Simms and Hutton. McCarter wanted to hit back and he was reasonably sure he could take both men at the same time. The smile on Simms's skinny face taunted McCarter, daring him to start swinging.

But McCarter did not intend to fight his SAS brethren. The terrorists inside the embassy were the enemy. Simms was just a pain in the arse and Hutton was his pet flunky. McCarter would have to tolerate the two bastards for the moment. He clenched his teeth and turned to face the wall, his body trembling with rage like a volcano about to erupt.

"Frisk him, Sergeant," Simms ordered. "McCarter has a thing about carrying weapons even when he's off duty. Check him careful now. Sneaky bloke knows all the tricks."

Hutton's hands patted down McCarter. The sergeant checked for ankle holsters and wrist knives. He probed the back of McCarter's neck and between his legs. Finally, the NCO announced that McCarter was clean.

"What's all this nonsense for?" McCarter asked wearily.

"Empty your pockets," Simms ordered. "Might have some sort of tear-gas pen or an explosive hidden in a cigarette pack."

"What a bunch of rot," McCarter muttered, but he obeyed instructions and removed all articles from his pockets, placing them on the nearest table.

"You seem to forget that I'm aware of the fact you left the SAS to become a cloak-and-dagger chap," Simms said sourly. "Didn't seem you were with Her Majesty's Secret Service, so I figure you're working for the American CIA. Unless you've defected by now. Could be with the Commies for all I know."

McCarter clenched his fists in helpless anger. Simms was trying to enrage him and the bastard was succeeding. Sergeant Hutton recognized the fury in McCarter's eyes. The NCO opened the button-flap holster on his hip in case he needed to draw his side arm.

"I came to try to help you blokes," McCarter explained. "After all, I participated in Nimrod. Unless my memory is faulty, I believe all your experience was pushing Irish civilians about in Belfast, Simms."

"You'll address the major as sir, McCarter," Hutton demanded.

"Look, mate," McCarter grated, his anger boiling to the brink of endurance. "You've shoved me about and been a bit heavy-handed, but I'm not really pissed at you yet. I reckon Simms has told you a lot of lying shit about me, so I don't blame you for your attitude. But don't push me too far."

"And just what the fuck do you think...?" Hutton began.

"Let's all relax a bit," Simms announced. The major was well aware that McCarter might explode if they continued to harass him. "McCarter wants to do us a favor. Seems to figure the SAS can't get along without him."

"It's possible I might come up with something you overlooked," McCarter replied. "I'm tired of trying to justify why I'm here and I'm tired of all the crap you're giving me, Simms. If you want to keep playing games, I may as well leave. Otherwise, let's talk about the embassy."

"We're not giving classified information to a sod who might be workin' for the bleedin' Russians," Hutton sneered.

"I wish you'd draw that gun on your hip," McCarter said with a wolfish grin. "Then I'd have an excuse to jam it up your arse and squeeze the trigger."

"I don't need a gun to take care of you!" Hutton snarled, unbuckling his belt.

"Sergeant!" Simms snapped. "You're a professional soldier. Behave accordingly."

"Sorry, sir," Hutton replied sheepishly. "But I'd dearly love to thrash this bastard."

"Put your belongings back in your pockets, McCarter," Simms invited as he opened a pewter cigarette case. "Want a smoke?"

"I have my own," McCarter replied. "Shall we talk about the embassy now?"

"Oh, we could take the embassy," Simms said with a shrug. "Although it wouldn't be as easy as Operation Nimrod."

"Nimrod wasn't exactly a cakewalk," McCarter commented, shaking a Player's from a cigarette case.

"But you only had a handful of terrorists led by that Iraqi fanatic who called himself Own to worry about," Simms explained. "There are more than thirty terrorists inside the Mardarajan embassy. Could be as many as fifty. And they're well armed too. Kalashnikovs, Heckler & Koch G34A assault rifles, Sterling MK4 submachine guns and at least one RPD light machine gun. That's not including explosives and handguns, which they've probably got in there as well."

"Must have had all that gear hidden in the luggage and furniture crates hauled into the embassy," McCarter mused.

"None of that stuff was checked because of diplomatic immunity," Simms said with exasperation. "That's the same reason we can't simply blast the bloody building to bits."

"Then there are no hostages inside?" McCarter asked.

"At first we thought they might be holding some Egyptians or Jordanians hostage," the major answered. "But we contacted those embassies and both the Egyptian and Jordanian ambassadors claim none of their people are missing."

"But there *are* Arabs in there as well as black Africans?" McCarter asked.

"That's a media rumor," Simms stated. "Hasn't been confirmed officially."

"In other words, you're not at liberty to tell me."

"Can't say one way or the other, McCarter." Simms shrugged. "It's an unconfirmed rumor. All right?"

"Fair enough," McCarter agreed. "The building appears to be only about half the size of the Iranian embassy. So, I reckon it has about twenty-five rooms."

"Give or take a loo," Simms answered. "We can't be sure, of course, but we think they're using most of the rooms as billets for the men. Others may be storage areas. They might have enough food and bottled water to last a month."

"Have the water and gas been cut off?" McCarter inquired.

"Yes." Simms nodded. "We're being a bit less civil with these bastards than we were with the Libyan embassy. After all, this incident is quite a bit worse already. We've also cut off the electricity, but they have some sort of generator in there. Probably petrol- or diesel-operated. The lights are on all the time. Bastards were prepared for this business."

"How well are you lads prepared?" McCarter asked.

"I assume you've already got snipers posted on rooftops and such."

"Naturally," Simms replied. "And we've got access to plenty of military force if needed. The Royal Marines already have a couple companies stationed around the building, and they'll send in an entire battalion if needed. Most of them have served urban security duty in Ulster, so they're experienced with antiterrorism. The Tenth Parachute Battalion also has a unit of 'Red Devils' on standby. So, we've got more than enough manpower and firepower to take the embassy, but our hands are tied by diplomatic immunity and concern about world opinion at the goddamn United Nations. How's that for nonsense?"

"Bloody awful," McCarter answered.

"For once we can agree about something, McCarter," Simms remarked as he crushed out a cigarette in an ashtray. "So the only help we really need is for someone to convince the prime minister and the home secretary to let us do our job."

"I'm afraid I don't have any influence in that direction," McCarter confessed. "Just thought I'd see if there was any way I could help, but I think you've got everything covered. That's a bloody shock. Didn't think you had it in you, Simms."

"We don't have any love for each other, McCarter," Simms commented. "And I won't pretend we don't still have a couple grudges against each other. You'll never admit it, but the way I handled my job in Belfast was the only way that will ever work in Northern Ireland. Right now, I have to handle this situation the way I'm allowed to, instead of the way it ought to be done."

"Be interesting to hear how things turn out," McCarter mused. "I'll be listening to the radio as much as possible to try to keep up with things."

"Radio?" Simms raised his eyebrows. "Sounds like you're planning to leave the country for a while. Another secret mission for the CIA, I expect."

"I can't say if I ever worked for the CIA or not." McCarter smiled. "But I've got a job to do with some chaps that isn't exactly an official action."

"I knew it." Simms clucked his tongue with disgust. "You've joined some sort of mercenary army, haven't you? I knew you'd eventually wind up becoming a damned soldier of fortune, McCarter. You were always too undisciplined, too much a maverick to be content with regular military service. Of course, a merc gets paid a hell of a lot better than us common troopers, eh?"

"No comment," McCarter replied simply. "I'd better be on my way now. Have fun with your crisis, Simms."

9

The other four members of Phoenix Force landed at Heathrow airport at eight-fifty that evening. They arrived on a commercial airliner and had to go through customs along with the other passengers. Forged passports and other identification passed all inspections without raising a single official eyebrow.

The four commandos hauled their suitcases to a taxicab in front of the airport. Manning slid into the seat beside the driver as Katz, Encizo and James climbed into the back.

"Let's see," the cabbie began, noticing the blue and gray business suits worn by the four strangers. One chap was black and another appeared to be a South American of some sort. The driver figured they were not related. Of course, you can never be sure about Yanks.

"You gents must be here on business, eh?" he asked.

"Basically," Manning replied. "But we hope to combine pleasure with business while we're here."

"London is the best city in the world for that, sir," the cabbie assured him. "You gents all Americans?"

"Yeah, we're All Americans, Jack," Calvin James said. "Two halfbacks, a quarterback and a coach."

"Oh," the cabbie replied lamely, unfamiliar with American sports. "Well, where do you gents want to go? The Hilton on Park Lane? If you haven't already got reservations, might I suggest White's on Lancaster Gate? The rooms cost less and you get a loverly view of Hyde Park. Staff is nice too...."

"We want to unwind a little first," Manning told him. "Do you know where the Golden Unicorn is?"

"That little pub on Stamford Street?" The driver nodded. "Very good, sir. Sit back and enjoy the ride."

"Spare us the scenic route," the Canadian told him. "We'll go sight-seeing later. We're in kind of a hurry now. Okay?"

"Right, guv," the cabbie assured him. "You'll think this cab has sprouted wings, I'll get you there so fast."

They arrived at the Golden Unicorn about half an hour later. The cabbie opened the boot of the taxi and everyone retrieved his luggage. Katzenelenbogen paid the driver and gave him a reasonable tip.

"So this is an English pub," James mused, gazing at a painting of a beer mug with a unicorn head jutting from the brim, on a shingle above the door.

"As seen on TV," Manning replied. "This is one of the numerous taverns McCarter took me to when I was here a couple of years ago."

"I didn't know you'd been here before," James remarked.

"Oh, yeah," the Canadian said. "McCarter conned me into entering a marathon race in Kent. Well, you know I'm a long-distance runner, right? McCarter is sure I can win and tells me how we'll rake in a small fortune with all the bets he's making on me. He went on and on with that crap, so I agreed to enter the race."

"Did you win?"

"I finished in first place," Manning answered. "Even though a couple local bastards tried to jump me when I was running through the woods. McCarter was watching for something like that. You know how he can sense danger.''

''And he always heads straight for it,'' Encizo added with a grin.

''Well, he bailed me out in the woods,'' the Canadian admitted. ''But then we went to a pub to collect our money and a bunch of Kentish sore losers refused to pay and accused *us* of cheating.''

''What happened?'' James asked.

''McCarter and I had to duke it out with everybody in the goddamn pub. Damn near got killed. That's the usual sort of good time you can expect when you socialize with David McCarter.''

''I know what you mean.'' Encizo laughed. ''David and I went out on the town once in Miami. He tried to pick up a blond in a bar. Turned out she was the mistress of the leader of a loan-sharking racket. So we had to punch out four or five gangsters. Then this other guy pulls a gun and McCarter hits him with a chair and knocks him out cold. Later on we found out the poor nerd was an undercover cop. One hell of a time.''

''David does have a way with people,'' Katz said dryly. ''Are you sure this is a good place to meet him, Gary?''

''I think so,'' Manning replied. ''I just hope we can get in touch with him. McCarter might be running around trying to get a safe house and making other arrangements for us.''

''Doesn't he have a regular contact who's associated with British intelligence?'' James inquired.

''A man named Hillerman.'' Katz nodded. ''Ordinarily, we could contact him, but we'd better not use a middleman in this case. The safest method might be the most direct and least complicated. Call him on the phone.''

"His home phone might be tapped," Encizo warned. "In fact, I'd be surprised if it isn't."

"I'll call him," Manning announced. "I think I can tell David where we are without giving the exact address. He'll figure it out, but anyone listening on a wiretap won't be able to put the pieces together until it's too late."

"Too late for who?" James asked with a frown.

"Get a table and keep an eye on my suitcase while I make the call, okay?" Manning insisted.

The other three entered the Golden Unicorn while the Canadian headed for a phone booth on the corner. The pub was fairly crowded. Several men sat at tables, drinking beer or ale as they chatted pleasantly together. Four patrons played darts. A mist of gray smoke hovered within the tavern like a pungent cloud. Encizo grimaced as he waved some pipe smoke away from his face.

"Haven't any of these guys ever heard of snuff?" the Cuban complained.

Katz and James selected a table near a wall, instinctively wanting to protect their backs while in a public place. Encizo took one of his suitcases and headed for the men's room.

Inside the loo, Encizo found a vacant stall and placed his case on the toilet. He closed the stall door and made certain it was securely latched before he opened the suitcase.

The Cuban took out his wallet and removed a plastic credit card. A phony VISA card printed in the name of Carlos Mendoza, it was more than just a forged document for Encizo's false identity. He snapped off the bottom of the card and inserted it into a tiny slot above the lining of the suitcase lid.

The plastic strip was actually a flat key. The numerals of the expiration date triggered a computer-programmed lock tumbler. A dull click signaled Encizo that the secret compartment was unlocked. He pulled on the lining and a section opened like a tiny door.

The computerized false bottom was one of the last innovations developed by the late Keio Ohara. The Japanese electronics expert had been the team gadgetsmaker as well as a superb warrior and trusted friend.

Encizo reached inside the compartment and removed a Gerber Mark I fighting dagger, a favorite of the Cuban Phoenix Force pro. A foil handle of cast aluminum, a full quillon and a five-inch double-edged steel blade made the Gerber an excellent close-quarters weapon.

The Cuban took the knife from its sheath and smiled as he examined it. He realized that his fondness for edged weapons might be considered a bit macaber by most, but the knife had been the first weapon he mastered.

Encizo returned the Gerber to its sheath and clipped it to his belt at the small of his back, concealing it under his jacket. The Cuban then reached into the compartment again and extracted two *shaken* throwing stars from the case.

The six-pointed steel stars were weapons, employed by students of *shuriken-jutsu*. Encizo had learned this martial art from the late Keio Ohara. The Cuban had easily mastered the *shaken*. He had learned how to accurately throw knives as a youth, although this skill has limited practical use. Nonetheless, Encizo's accuracy with the star-shaped weapons rivaled the talents of the fabled *ninja* espionage agents and assassins of feudal Japan.

The Cuban slipped the *shaken* into his coat pockets and closed and locked the suitcase. He emerged from the loo and joined Katz and James at the table. Three mugs of red beer and a glass of wine arrived as Encizo pulled up a chair.

"There you go, gents," a heavy-set barman announced, placing the drinks on the table. "One pound and fifty pence, please."

"How much is that in real money?" James wondered aloud.

"British currency is real money, sir," the barman said stiffly.

"I have some real money for you," Katz assured him, placing a pound note and several coins on the table.

"Thank you, sir," the barman said, surprised to discover Katz had paid him with shillings instead of the current pence coins. No matter. Shillings were still valid in the United Kingdom.

"You feel better since you visited the head, Rafael?" James whispered as the barman returned to his station.

"I'm never comfortable without my knife," the Cuban confessed. "I'd feel even better if I'd been able to smuggle a gun into the country as well."

"We had to make this trip on short notice," Katz commented. "It was difficult enough to take care of the forged identification papers in time to make the earliest possible flight to London. Hopefully, McCarter will be able to supply us with firearms and other gear we'll need for the mission."

"And hopefully we'll get back to the States before Brognola finds out about this," James added.

"Dream on, amigo," Encizo said dryly. "Nobody can keep a secret from Stony Man. Not even us. I wouldn't be surprised if Brognola already knows we left the States."

"And he'll probably figure out where we went,"

Katz stated. His left hand raised the glass of wine to his lips. The Israeli wore pearl-gray gloves. Unless one noticed the fingers of his right hand were unusually rigid, one would not suspect it was a prosthesis.

"Yeah," Encizo agreed. "If Hal doesn't put two and two together by just listening to the evening news, Kurtzman and his computers will figure it out. Those guys are the best in the business at what they do."

"I'm surprised they haven't tracked down Bolan by now," James mused.

"I'm not," Katz said with a smile. "Brognola and Kurtzman *don't want* to track down Bolan. Even if the President forced them to do it, I'm sure they wouldn't help the headhunters who are after the Executioner. They'd probably give the White House misinformation based on outdated data if the Oval Office gets pushy."

"Even if they locate the Executioner," Encizo added, "they'll never get him by sending the CIA or conventional commandos after him. The only people who could capture the Executioner alive would be Able Team or Phoenix Force. We won't turn against Mack and Brognola knows it."

"I know Bolan is good," James said. "But sooner or later somebody is gonna catch up with him. I agree, they won't take him alive. Whenever the spooks find Bolan—whether the hit team is sent by Moscow or Washington—they'll kill him."

"The Executioner isn't an easy man to kill," Encizo said with a shrug. "He can take care of himself and we've got our own problems."

"Yeah," James muttered. "We're gonna catch hell when we go back to the States."

"It won't be as bad as the other time we decided to take on an unauthorized assignment in Israel," Katz assured him. "That was right after the Executioner parted company with Stony Man. Besides, I'd rather get lectured by Brognola and criticized by the President than refuse to respond to a call for help from a fellow member of Phoenix Force.''

"I remember what Keio said when we were in Israel,'' the Cuban remarked. '' 'Phoenix Force is supposed to fight terrorism. Our duty is more important than who orders us to the task.' ''

"Well,'' James said with a sigh. "I'm not about to argue that. I agreed to come on this mission and I knew the score when I accepted. Still, I hope this doesn't turn out to be our *last* mission because the White House decides to pull the plug on Phoenix Force.''

Gary Manning entered the Golden Unicorn pub. He found his partners and headed for the table. James looked up at the Canadian as he sipped is beer.

"Yech,'' the black man rasped, putting down his mug. "The British really *do* drink warm beer.''

"You should have brought along an ice chest,'' Manning remarked as he sunk into a chair.

"Did you get in touch with David?'' Encizo inquired.

"Yeah,'' the Canadian said as he nodded. "I told him I was Tom Horn and I just rode into London on a big yellow horse.''

"I see.'' Katz rolled his eyes toward the ceiling. "You think McCarter will put 'Horn' and 'yellow horse' together and come up with the Golden Unicorn.''

"Well,'' Manning began, "I also told him I was hanging around the local saloon.''

"We might be hanging around here all night before David figures out a message like that,'' James groaned.

"What did David say when you told him this clever little code?'' Encizo asked dryly.

"He said he didn't care if I was Tom Horn or Jesse

James and hung up," the Canadian answered sheepishly.

"Excuse me, gentlemen," the barman announced. "Could you fellows drink up, please? We're closing the pub in about ten more minutes, mates."

"What?" James glanced at a clock above the bar. "It isn't even ten o'clock yet."

"That's normal closing time for an English pub," Katz explained. "London isn't a late-night city. A few discos are open until three in the morning, but most taverns don't stay open until 2:00 A.M. like they do in the States."

"Guess we'll have to wait outside," Encizo remarked.

"What are we gonna do if McCarter doesn't figure out what Tom Horn and his yellow horse means?" James inquired.

"He will," Manning insisted. "It was a good clue. You'll see."

"Uh-huh," James replied without enthusiasm.

10

A heavy fog drifted across Stamford Street. Katz turned up the collar of his trench coat as the clammy mist settled in. Accustomed to warm climates, Encizo began to pace, gently beating his arms against his torso for warmth.

"How long have we been waiting out here?" the Cuban asked, gazing up at the blurred light of a street lamp, distorted by the blanket of fog.

"Twenty-five minutes," James replied, checking his wristwatch. "Hey, Tom Horn. How's your yellow horse, man?"

"It was a good clue," Manning answered, a trace of annoyance in his tone. He placed his suitcase on the sidewalk, but kept a briefcase in his right hand. "Could you have come up with anything better?"

"Yeah," James answered, but he didn't volunteer any examples.

"I hate this weather," Encizo complained. "I haven't felt this miserable since we were in Alaska a couple of years ago."

"We'll wait five more minutes," Katz suggested. "Then we'll see about a hotel and...."

Footsteps clapped the concrete. Several shapes gradually materialized amid the fog. Heads and shoulders formed. Young faces appeared. Some wore beards or shoulder-length hair. They were male, yet several wore eye shadow and rouge. A few had dyed their hair purple or green. Two wore safety pins for earrings and one had a similar item of jewelry attached to his right nostril.

There were nine of them. Nine nasty young men who had rebelled against a society that had protected and provided for them. They had rejected a culture that tolerated their antiestablishment behavior. The right to be different was not enough for these particular punks. They had created their own culture with primitive rules and selfish values.

"Oh, shit," Calvin James whispered as the young toughs approached.

"What have we got here, mates?" chuckled a shaggy youth clad in an imitation leather jacket with a pattern of metal studs along the shoulders and sleeves.

"Looks like Yank tourists waitin' for a cab," snickered a punk with purple hair cut in a Mohawk fashion. "Never find one in this pea soup, gents."

"Not likely a bobby is going to happen along either," a beefy hood commented as he unwound a chain from his belt. "So you fellas had best not give us any trouble."

"You guys don't know what trouble is," Encizo remarked, slipping a hand into a coat pocket.

"You think you're tough, laddie?" the shaggy leader grinned. He pressed the button of an oblong object in his right fist. A six-inch blade snapped open. "Not as tough as steel."

"Look," Gary Manning said, sighing. "We don't want any trouble. How about a deal? We'll pay you a hundred dollars to leave us alone."

"A hundred dollars?" The purple-haired freak laughed. "You must be daft!"

"That comes to about eleven dollars and ten cents for each of you guys," James commented. "Not bad wages for five minutes' work."

"We're through talkin'," the gang leader announced. "We're takin' everything you Yank bastards have. You can either hand everything over without a struggle, or we'll do this the hard way."

"Hard for you, boy," Katz warned. "If you take one more step, I'll kill you."

The hoodlum leader whirled to face Katz. The Israeli had extended his right arm and pointed the gloved index finger at the young thud. The gang leader laughed at this absurd gesture.

"You senile old bastard," he snorted. "I'm going to teach you. . . ."

Orange flame burst from the tip of Katz's finger. The digit was actually the barrel of a single-shot pistol built into his prosthesis. The gang leader's head bounced violently as a .22 Magnum projectile struck between his eyebrows. The youth's eyes rolled upward as his knees buckled. He tumbled into a gutter, his body twitching slightly while the last traces of life seeped from his carcass.

"Bloody fuck!" the purple-headed thug exclaimed.

Rafael Encizo's arm suddenly whirled as he unleashed a *shaken* throwing-star. The weapon slammed into the punk's face. He stumbled backward, the *shaken* lodged in his forehead. Two tines penetrated the skull bone to pierce his brain. The hoodlum collapsed and joined his leader in the gutter.

"Get 'em!" a young tough shouted as he drew an ice pick from a boot sheath. "Kill the blighters!"

The iceman attacked Calvin James, executing a rapier-lunge for the black man's stomach. James's cobra-quick reflexes sent him into action. His right leg became a blur as he swung a roundhouse kick. The junior thug cried out when James's foot smashed into his hand, striking the ice pick from numb fingers.

James whirled with the motion of his kick, pivoted in a circle and slashed his left foot backward. The heel caught his opponent between the legs. A gasping whine escaped from the punk's gaping mouth as he clasped both hands to his crotch.

The black warrior did not give the British J.D. time to recover. He lashed the back of his right fist across the punk's jaw, followed by a left hook. The hood dropped faster than the price of ice cubes in Alaska.

James saw something move out of the corner of his eye. A knuckle-duster-clad fist rocketed toward his face. The black man barely dodged the deadly punch in time to avoid a bone-breaking experience. The fist-flinging hoodlum moved well. His arm slashed a fast cross-body stroke and chopped the knuckle-duster into James's midsection.

The black man grunted from the blow. His opponent's left fist shot out and tagged James's chin. The Phoenix Force pro staggered two steps back. He was glad the thug did not wear knuckle-dusters on both hands.

The hoodlum swung another steel-clad fist at the black man's head, hoping to put him out of action with the next blow. James danced out of the path of the fist and immediately snapped a tae kwon-do kick to the thug's lower abdomen. The British lowlife doubled up. James seized the wrist behind the knuckle-dusters and twisted his opponent's arm.

James's leg flashed again, driving another kick to the thug's battered belly. The youth convulsed in a retching gasp. James's hand slashed a karate chop to the nape of his opponent's neck. The hoodlum fell face first to the pavement, the cartilage in his nose crunching on impact.

The muscle-bound goon armed with a length of chain

attacked Gary Manning. The Canadian raised his valise for a shield and blocked the steel links. Before the hood could swing his chain again, Manning charged the bullyboy and rammed the briefcase into the hood's chest.

The thug stumbled backward, but managed to retain his balance. Manning chopped the edge of his valise across the guy's wrist. The chain slipped from the ape's grasp. Manning backhanded the case across his opponent's face. The hood's cloth hat whirled off his square head as he fell on his backside, blood bubbling from a broken nose.

Another gang member, armed with a tire iron, swung his weapon at the Canadian. Again, Manning's valise protected him from the murderous assault, but the force of the blow knocked the case out of Manning's hands. The hood with the tire iron grinned as he raised his metal cudgel once more.

Manning's foot lashed out, delivering a low side kick to his opponent's kneecap. Bone and cartilage cracked as the joint burst apart. The thug screamed in pain and anger as he blindly swung the iron. Manning sidestepped, and the weapon-tool rang against the pavement.

The Canadian's foot stamped the iron, pinning it to the ground. Manning quickly clasped both hands together and brought them down hard, chopping the young villain at the base of the neck. The youth fell unconscious, but the chain man was back on his feet and ready to go another round with the Phoenix Force warrior.

The hoodlum had retrieved his cap and held it in a clenched fist. The thug attacked Manning and swung a cross-body swipe at the Canadian's face. Manning raised an arm to ward off the blow. Sharp metal split the sleeve and sliced a narrow furrow in Manning's forearm. The Canadian jumped back, startled by the unexpected sting.

"Son of a bitch," Manning rasped when he realized he was bleeding.

The thug had razor blades sewn into the bill of his cap. He smiled and stepped closer to try another slash with his deadly headgear. Manning shuffled away from the attack, nearly tripping over a suitcase.

As his adversary prepared to charge, the Canadian stepped around the luggage and his foot swept into the suitcase, kicking it like a soccer ball. The case hurled off the ground and crashed into the thug's torso.

Although the blow caused no physical harm, it surprised and disoriented the hoodlum. Manning closed in fast. He swung his right fist into the goon's face as his left hand seized the guy's arm behind the hat.

The fingers of Manning's right hand grabbed the thug's shaggy locks, and he pulled the punk's head forward and shoved the creep's own hat under his chin. The razor blades sliced flesh. Blood poured from a deep wound in the hoodlum's throat. Manning released the punk and allowed him to slump to the pavement where he continued to die in a thrashing heap.

A knife-wielding youth had launched himself at Rafael Encizo. The Cuban dodged the lunge and drew his Gerber Mark I. The British punk whirled and attempted a backhand slash, but Encizo was too skilled and experienced with a blade to be taken off guard by such a fundamental tactic.

The Cuban's knife raked the hoodlum's upper arm, cutting into the triceps muscle. The youth screamed as his hand popped open, dropping his switchblade. He backed away from Encizo, eyes wide with terror. The Cuban smiled thinly and stepped back. He casually kicked the kid's knife across the pavement. It slid six feet to stop in front of the startled youth.

"Pick it up, *chico*," Encizo invited.

The punk hesitated for a moment and bent over to retrieve his weapon. Encizo stepped forward and kicked the kid in the face. The youth tumbled across the sidewalk and lay unconscious, a purple bruise mushrooming on his broken jaw.

Only two of the gang members were still on their feet. One young savage, no smarter than his comrades, attacked Yakov Katzenelenbogen, swinging a hickory cudgel at the Israeli's head.

Katz's right arm swept a fast roundhouse stroke. The steel hand slapped the cudgel, swatting it out of the punk's grasp. The Israeli superpro quickly backhanded the prosthesis across the kid's face. The youth's lips split and blood trickled down his chin. He swayed and stumbled, but Katz's left hand snaked out and seized the punk's denim vest.

The Phoenix Force commander bent his right elbow and thrust his prosthesis like a knight's lance. The tips of the steel "fingers" plunged into the hoodlum's solar plexus. A variation of a karate *nukite* stroke, the blow ruptured the youth's main internal organ. Eighteen years old, the kid suffered a fatal heart attack and landed at Katz's feet.

The ninth and final member of the street gang had held back while his companions locked horns with Phoenix Force. He was glad he had done so. The four "tourists" had chopped down all his mates in less than half a minute. The youth had no desire to share the same fate as the others. He bolted into the fog, praying that the mysterious warriors in business suits would not follow.

The panic-stricken hoodlum failed to notice the twin

beams of light that knifed through the fog. A horn blared a harsh warning as tires squealed to an abrupt halt. The car stopped only inches from the terrified youth, but the punk was too preoccupied with flight to appreciate how close he came to a bone-crunching encounter with the street machine.

"You bloody idiot!" the driver shouted at the fleeing figure. "You'd better go home and put your brain in, you silly sod!"

"Thank God," Katz said, sighing, "it's McCarter. I'd recognize that bellow anywhere."

"I told you he'd show up," Manning declared.

McCarter's BMW pulled up to the curb. He parked the car and opened a door. The British ace strained his eyes to peer through the dense gray mist. He smiled when he recognized his Phoenix Force brethren.

"Welcome to London, mates," he announced. McCarter raised his eyebrows when he noticed the unconscious and dead bodies sprawled across the pavement. "Looks like you've already gotten to know a few of the local chaps."

"Yeah," James replied sourly. "And your taxi service sucks, man."

"It's not so easy driving in this fog, mate," McCarter replied. "Besides, I had some trouble with Gary's message. I went to the Yellow Mare Pub on Horn Street before I came here."

"It was still a good clue," Manning said stubbornly.

"Let's get the hell out of here and talk later," Katz urged. "We don't want to be here when the police arrive."

11

McCarter told his partners about the Mardarajan embassy as he drove the BMW through the fog-filled streets of London. The other members of Phoenix Force were not surprised to learn the embassy was the target site of their mission, but they were disappointed that McCarter had little information about the incident that had not already been reported by UPI.

"You say there are approximately forty terrorists inside the embassy?" Katz inquired as he pulled the powder-burnt glove from his prosthetic hand. "And they all appear to be armed with full-auto weapons?"

"That's right," the Briton confirmed. "Hell, we've taken on tougher jobs in the past."

"Five men against forty aren't real good odds, David," Manning told him. "If you knew how to count, you'd realize that."

"We've faced worse odds," McCarter insisted. "Remember the time we tangled with those Red Anvil fanatics in the Atlantic? What about Krio Island and Kaplan's Castle?"

"We didn't have to operate entirely on our own either," Encizo reminded him. "Even in Israel we had help."

"We didn't have to get past an area surrounded by Royal Marines, British police and SAS commandos either," Katz added. "Before we can hit the embassy we'll have to penetrate the security net of police and soldiers that surrounds the building. That won't be easy. The London police force is one of the best in the world. The Royal Marines are hardly a bunch of inexperienced trainees. I don't even want to think about going up against the SAS.''

"Don't you know the dude in charge of the SAS at the embassy, David?" James asked.

"Damn right I know him," the Briton replied gruffly. "Major Simms is the sorriest excuse for a field-grade officer that ever dishonored Great Britain by failing to die at birth.''

"I bet he loves you too," Manning said dryly.

"We share a deep-rooted mutual hatred for each other," McCarter confirmed as he steered the BMW onto the Lambeth Bridge over the Thames River. "I first met Simms in 1981. He was Captain Simms at the time, company commander in charge of an antiterrorist unit to oppose the IRA urban guerrillas in Northern Ireland. The minute I laid eyes on Simms, I knew the bastard would be trouble. Lord knows, he turned out to be that.''

"What did he do?" Encizo asked with a grin. "Catch you drunk on sentry duty?''

"No," McCarter said in a hard voice. "Simms decided the best way to find out where IRA terrorists were hiding was to interrogate Catholic civilians. He found a couple of Protestant bullyboys, bigoted thugs who Simms figured would agree to go along with his Gestapo tactics. Of course, he didn't tell anyone in the SAS what he was up to. None of us knew about it until I happened upon one of these inquisitions. I was on patrol when I heard a woman scream from a cottage.

"I headed to the house to investigate," McCarter continued, his voice tense with anger as memories flooded into his mind with painful clarity. "I found

Simms and his pet thugs inside. The bullies had strapped a middle-aged woman to a chair. Her face was bruised and bloodied. The front of her dress had been ripped open to expose her breasts. The goons had a manually operated generator set up on a table close by. Alligator clips were attached to her nipples. Wires connected the poor woman to that infernal machine as the bastards took turns at the crank.''

"Did Simms torture her too?'' James asked.

"He did not personally participate,'' McCarter answered. "But he certainly didn't try to stop it. Bastard was calmly smoking a cigarette while he watched his lads torture the woman.''

"Christ, David,'' Manning muttered. "What did you do?''

"I ran inside and slammed the butt of my rifle into one bastard's face and kicked him in the jewels before he could fall,'' McCarter replied. "The other son of a bitch pulled a pistol from his belt. That was fine with me because it gave me the right to shoot him right between the eyes.''

"What did you do about Simms?'' James inquired.

"Well,'' the Briton said with a shrug, "I couldn't just shoot a British officer, so I forced him to strip off his gun belt and tunic. Then I marched him outside, laid down my rifle and kicked his rotten arse all over Belfast.''

"You're lucky you weren't court-martialed,'' James commented.

"Oh, there was a court-martial,'' McCarter explained. "It was virtually a state secret, of course. No one wanted to publicly announce that a British field-grade was charged with committing atrocities in Northern Ireland. I was surprised by the way Simms confessed to 'bending a few rules,' although he denied ordering the goons to torture anyone. 'Things got a bit out of hand,' he said. Well, charges were dropped against me for striking an officer. Simms was quietly transferred to a regular army unit.''

''But he's back in the SAS now,'' Encizo said with a frown.

''I don't know how that awful mistake happened.'' McCarter sighed. ''Unfortunately, Simms has been back with the SAS for about two years now. I know that because the bastard was sent to deliver a message to me once. Bloody sod broke into my flat while I was asleep. I don't know what he was trying to prove by that stunt. Probably hoped he'd catch me off guard so he could report that I'd lost my edge. As it turned out, I woke up and jumped Simms before I knew who he was. Damn near strangled him. Rather wish I had now.''

''It doesn't sound like we can expect any cooperation from Simms,'' Katz commented. ''That means we'll have to find some other way to get past the security forces. Any suggestions, David?''

''I've seen the setup at the embassy,'' McCarter answered. ''Security is tight. Very tight. Maybe Major Hillerman can help us find a way into the building.''

''Where are we going now?'' Manning inquired, staring at the fog that surrounded the BMW.

''To see a fellow about some hardware,'' the Briton explained, steering the car onto Grosvenor Road.

He soon pulled into an alley beside a building with two bicycles and a moped in a display window. A sign above the door bore the legend, Spokes Unlimited.

''Looks like a bicycle shop,'' James commented.

''It is,'' McCarter answered as he turned off the engine. ''But Felix Holmes has another business that he doesn't publicize.''

''Oh, God,'' Manning muttered. ''Another one of your wacko friends.''

"Right," the Briton replied cheerfully as he opened the door to emerge from the car. "You chaps will get along famously with him."

FELIX HOLMES looked like a character actor preparing to play Rasputin in a movie. Six foot five, with a dense black beard and pale, almost transparent green eyes, Holmes was a formidable and bizarre-looking fellow. However, he warmly welcomed McCarter and the other members of Phoenix Force, pumping everyone's hand as they entered the bicycle shop, like a vicar greeting his congregation after a service.

"David told me to expect you gents," Holmes explained, a trace of Gloucester in his voice. "I'm sure we'll enjoy doing business together."

"Exactly what business are you referring to, Mr. Holmes?" Katz inquired.

"Just call me Felix," the big Briton replied. "And I assume you're not interested in bikes and such. My unofficial business is the sale of . . . uh, equipment for personal protection, you might say."

"You're a gunrunner?" Encizo asked.

"That's an unpleasant term." Holmes frowned. "But essentially correct."

"Show them your armory, Felix," McCarter urged.

"Of course," Holmes said with a grin. "Follow me to the hardware section, gentlemen."

Holmes escorted his guests through the bike shop. Wheels, handlebars and bicycle frames hung on the walls like big-game trophies. The gunrunner opened a closet door. Inside, a false back, which served as a secret door, stood open.

"Ordinarily I've got a bunch of shelves with tools and such in this closet," Holmes explained. "Hides this secret passage nicely that way. Just like an old movie on the telly. The door leads to a cellar that isn't mentioned in the official blueprints. Love this business. Everything is official and unofficial—which means I keep a lot of my activities a secret from the authorities. Don't have to pay taxes on them either. Love that part of it. . . ."

The gunrunner led the men of Phoenix Force down a flight of stairs as he spoke. The basement was an armory with columns of racks filled with weapons and crates of ammunition. Holmes continued to chat away like a real-estate salesman as he escorted the visitors through the covert arms room.

"Here we go, gentlemen," Holmes announced proudly. "Automatic weapons on the left. Submachine guns and related subjects on the right. Handguns, shotguns and other items are at the back of the room."

"This is quite a collection," Manning commented as he examined the subguns. "British Sterlings, French MATs and West German H&Ks. Impressive."

"And none of them can be traced," Holmes declared. "Take a good look at those Sterlings and the H&Ks. You won't find a single serial number on any one of those weapons. See, the parts were. . . confiscated, shall we say, from the factories where they're made. Not a single part has a number stamped on it. Bloody beautiful, eh?"

"You must have an interesting network of friends," Calvin James commented. His mouth fell open when he noticed several M-16 assault rifles. "How the hell did you get these?"

"I didn't rob an American military base, if that's what has you worried," Holmes assured him. "But some of your own countrymen must have. Probably back in the States, I imagine."

"What do you mean?" James asked with a frown.

"Well," the gunrunner began, "you see, those rifles—along with an assortment of handguns, grenades, explosives and ammunition—were supposed to be delivered to the IRA. Some Irish-American sympathizers in the U.S. sent the stuff. However, my friends found out about the arms shipment and decided the bloody IRA didn't deserve such nice American-made guns.''

"You've got a number of Soviet-made AK-47s and AKMs here too,'' Encizo observed. ''Did you get them the same way?''

''Yes, indeed,'' Holmes confirmed. ''Moscow sends a lot of weapons to terrorist groups throughout Western Europe. When I find out about one of these shipments, it's my patriotic duty to prevent the guns from falling into the hands of such radicals. Of course, I may as well make a profit by selling the weapons afterward. I'm sure all of you believe in the free enterprise system, right?''

''As long as you don't want an outrageous price for your merchandise,'' Katz replied as he examined an Uzi subgun. ''How much for this weapon?''

''Two hundred and fifty British pounds sterling,'' the gunrunner answered.

''Price is too high,'' the Israeli said with a sigh.

''Felix reduces prices when customers buy in bulk,'' McCarter said. ''You realize, Felix, we need to purchase quite a bit of hardware.''

''All right,'' Holmes said with a shrug. ''I'll sell that Uzi for two hundred pounds, but don't expect me to go any lower than that. Hell of a deal, mate. See, I throw in five spare magazines and two hundred pounds of nine-millimeter ammo as accessories.''

''Sounds fine.'' Katz nodded. ''What sort of handguns do you have in stock?''

''Only the best,'' Holmes said with a smile. ''Got some American Smith & Wesson revolvers in .38 and

.357 Magnum. Also have some Colt revolvers and a few Army .45 automatics. Of course, I also have David's Belgium sweetheart in stock—the FN Browning Hi-Power. Sold you quite a few Brownings over the years, eh, mate?''

"I've used Felix's merchandise quite a few times in the past," McCarter told his companions. "He's never sold me any junk and he's always kept his mouth shut about our business."

"Okay," Manning said, "what about explosives, Felix?"

"That depends on what you need," Holmes answered. "If you mean grenades, I've got fragmentation types, stunners, tear-gas and some thermite."

"How about plastique?" the Canadian demolitions expert wanted to know.

"RDX compounds." The gunrunner nodded. "I've got about ten pounds of C-4. Familiar with the stuff?"

"I've used it once or twice," Manning assured him. "Do you happen to have any CV-38 low-velocity plastique?"

"You're in luck," Holmes said, grinning. "I believe I do at that. What else will you gents need?"

"We're not sure about that yet," McCarter replied. "We're not quite sure how to go about our mission just yet. When we've got a better idea what equipment we'll need, we'll be sure to buy it from you, Felix."

"Any way I can be of service, mate," the gunrunner said with an exaggerated bow.

"I'm glad you put it that way, Felix," McCarter commented with a smile. "See, we might need your personal assistance. The mission will be here in London."

"Wait one bloody minute, McCarter," Holmes said sharply. "I'm not a bleedin' commando or a mercenary or whatever the hell you blokes call yourselves. I'm a businessman. You have a demand for merchandise and I supply it. You can't ask for more than that."

"We don't ask it, dear fellow," McCarter insisted, placing a hand on the gunrunner's shoulder. "Your country is asking for your help, Felix. It's your duty as a good Englishman to participate in this mission."

"It's not my duty to get myself killed, damn you," Holmes snapped.

"We'll see to it that there will be only a minimum of risk involved in whatever tasks we assign you to," Katz promised.

"Minimum?" The gunrunner rolled his eyes toward the ceiling. "What do bloody lunatics like you five consider a minimum of risk? Dodging bullets instead of trying to catch them in your teeth?"

"The decision is up to you," the Israeli said with a shrug. "Of course, we would have paid you for your trouble...."

"Paid?" Holmes asked with interest. "How much?"

"Loyalty should be rewarded," Encizo stated. "A dedicated soldier deserves more than medals and verbal praise. Too bad you can't help."

"Well, now," Holmes began. "If crown and country need me, then I can't very well refuse."

"I knew we could count on your sense of patriotism," McCarter said dryly.

12

"President Skrubu," the prime minister spoke into the telephone as she drummed her fingers along the ink blotter on her desk. "I wish you would reconsider...."

"In other words, you think I should obey your orders because you are the head of the government of the United Kingdom," Skrubu's voice replied from the earpiece. "This is not the eighteenth century, Madame Prime Minister. You British can no longer dictate terms to Africans. As the president of Mardaraja, I find your pompous imperialism an insult to all the people of my country and to the black race throughout the world."

"This is not a racial issue, Mr. President," the prime minister insisted. "Nor am I trying to dictate terms of any kind. I am merely requesting that you give us permission to take immediate and direct action against the terrorists who have seized control of the Mardarajan embassy here in London."

"You want me to give permission for you to murder my people?" Skrubu scoffed. "I will not authorize you to invade Mardarajan territory and slaughter my subjects. Must I remind you, any act of aggression by your stormtroopers will be regarded as an act of war according to international law."

"We don't want to kill anyone." The prime minister sighed. "May I remind *you* that four British citizens have been murdered by the terrorists inside your embassy?"

"Ambassador Mafuta and his staff are not terrorists," Skrubu snapped. "Although you probably consider all black Africans as savages."

"Stop twisting what I say in order to distort the meaning," the prime minister told him. "If you aren't willing to let us deal with the terrorists, perhaps you'll agree to talk to Ambassador Mafuta. We'll establish a telephone link with the overseas line so you'll be able to speak with him directly. If Mafuta is not in league with the terrorists then he'll have nothing to fear from us. We'll cooperate with Mafuta if he'll cooperate with us. We only want the individuals involved in the shooting."

"You want my people to surrender to your military?"

"I want them to lay down their arms and turn themselves over to the police so we can investigate this matter and find out exactly who is responsible for the killings."

"To be tried in a British court of law by British subjects who hunger for revenge?" Skrubu demanded. "I will not order my people to surrender themselves to your kangaroo court."

"May I ask why you insist on protecting these terrorists, sir?" the PM asked, her voice strained from trying to control her anger. "Surely, you don't approve of what they've done."

"You mean what the English media and other Western press claim," Skrubu replied. "Of course, you wouldn't admit that the British secret service killed four Englishmen in order to create this propaganda against Mardaraja."

"That's absurd," the prime minister hissed through her teeth. "I haven't heard such outrageous nonsense since Khaddafi made a similar accusation during that Libyan embassy business last year."

"Colonel Khaddafi is a devout Muslim, a military leader and a man of principles," the African president declared. "I believe his word is more reliable than the ramblings of a hysterical female."

The prime minister had heard such insults before. Indeed, as the first woman to hold her office, she was accustomed to such remarks. The prime minister laughed at the comments that were made in jest and generally allowed nasty remarks to roll off her back. Skrubu was trying to irritate her and she would not give him the satisfaction of succeeding.

"So you and Colonel Khaddafi have patched up your differences and renewed your friendship," the PM said in a casual manner, as if discussing friends at a tea party. "But you two never really had a falling-out. I see now that you and Khaddafi planned this all along. You criticized each other in public while you conspired together. That explains the Arab terrorists at the embassy. Khaddafi must not trust your people so he sent some Libyans along to keep everyone in line. Does the colonel have you on a leash as well?"

"I will not be insulted by an English trollop," Skrubu snapped. "It is obvious your nation and mine will not be able to continue diplomatic relations, Madame Prime Minister."

"You're severing relations with the United Kingdom?"

"Yes," Skrubu confirmed. "There will be no need for you to send your ambassador to Mardaraja because we will not construct a British embassy here. Any British subject who enters this country will be arrested for espionage. We execute spies in Mardaraja, you know."

"And we have been known to kill terrorists here in England," the prime minister warned. "Since diplomatic relations have been officially severed, your people have forty-eight hours to evacuate the embassy and leave Great Britain.''

"Do you promise that my people will be able to leave the embassy unmolested and will be given safe passage back to Mardaraja?''

"If they leave within forty-eight hours," she replied. "Otherwise, I'll feel perfectly justified in ordering the SAS and the Royal Marines to tear the embassy apart— and to do the same to anyone inside it. Is that understood, Mr. President?''

"I demand a direct telephone link to the embassy in order to speak with Ambassador Mafuta," Skrubu declared. "I want to be certain my people understand this situation.''

"Very well, Mr. President," the prime minister replied. "Please hold the line and give us a minute or two to establish the link.''

AMBASSADOR MAFUTA received a telephone call at his office inside the Mardarajan embassy. President Skrubu personally delivered the message concerning the results of his conference with the British prime minister. Mafuta listened carefully and assured the president he understood the situation. Skrubu wished him luck and hung up.

Mafuta's hand trembled as he returned the telephone receiver to its cradle. He took a deep breath, trying to calm his racing heart. However, Major Hizam and Captain Nyoka stood in front of Mafuta's desk, waiting to learn about the phone call.

"That was President Skrubu," the ambassador explained. "Diplomatic relations between Mardaraja and Great Britain have been severed. We have to be out of here and on a plane back to Africa within forty-eight hours.''

"Good," Nyoka remarked, taking a pack of cigarettes from his pocket. "I'll be glad to get out of this place. Being surrounded by British soldiers isn't my idea of a vacation."

"You're being well paid, Captain," Hizam commented dryly.

"And I've earned every dinar, Major," Nyoka replied, lighting a cigarette. "Don't forget, I took care of Admiral Harker. That old fox might have ruined everything if I hadn't...."

"I'm certain you can find a mirror in the loo," Hizam said. "Why don't you watch your lips move while you congratulate yourself?"

"Just see to it I receive the rest of my money," Nyoka told the Libyan. "You might love to serve Khaddafi, but my politics are determined solely by how I can make a personal profit."

"Don't quarrel now," Mafuta pleaded. "Let's just pack up and get out of here before the British change their minds...."

"Not yet," Hizam said sternly. "We have forty-eight hours. That means we'll be safe until the time limit runs out."

"Why delay?" Mafuta asked, horrified by the Libyan's statement. "The longer we wait, the greater our chance of being attacked by the English."

"The English won't raid the embassy unless we fail to meet the deadline," Hizam insisted. "But we must not leave too quickly. The British will need time to prepare an airplane to take us to Africa."

"That's right," Nyoka was forced to agree. "We don't want to be waiting at the airport for the English to finish getting the jet ready when the bomb goes off here at the embassy."

"Must we use those explosives?" Mafuta asked

lamely, already aware of the answer. "The British have already been humiliated by this incident. Several Englishmen are dead and we've certainly embarrassed the government. The bomb is hardly necessary."

"You are not in charge of this mission," Hizam snapped. "Your position as ambassador is just a figurehead. Don't forget that, Mafuta. This is a Libyan operation. Mardaraja is merely an extension of Colonel Khaddafi's empire."

"And Khaddafi wants as many dead Englishmen as possible?" Mafuta shook his head. "That's insane."

"It is retribution," Hizam said angrily. "Your job is to follow orders, not to evaluate them. Don't forget that, Mafuta. And don't forget that you're expendable."

"I wish you two would calm down," Nyoka announced with a sly smile. "You should try to think about things the way I do. Life is really much more simple that way."

"Think like a mercenary?" Hizam spit with contempt. "A hired killer with no political conscience."

"That's right," Nyoka declared, no apology in his tone. "Major, you puff out our chest and brag about your devotion to Colonel Khaddafi and whatever righteous cause you think you're fighting for. Don't expect me to do the same. Hell, you talk about Khaddafi the way Jino talks about his leopard god. I don't give a damn about Khaddafi or Libya. This is just a job to me. That's all."

"It doesn't bother you to kill innocent people?" Mafuta inquired grimly.

"Innocent people get killed all the time," Nyoka said with a shrug. "They're involved in car accidents and plane crashes. They're victims of volcanoes and earthquakes."

"Accidental death is not the same as murder," Mafuta stated.

"Dead is dead," Nyoka declared. "When did you get so damn moralistic, Mafuta? Don't tell me you believe in God or life after death? Are you afraid of some sort of divine punishment for your sins in this world?"

"Of course not," Mafuta replied, but he was not certain whether he believed in a spiritual next life or not.

"Societies and governments set up rules of conduct," Nyoka continued. "They tell us murder is wrong. Yet governments cause wars. Hitler, Stalin and Mao killed millions of innocent people as part of their state policies. You're worried about a couple of hundred Englishmen?"

"I didn't participate in genocide by tyrants in Europe or China," Mafuta answered.

"No," Nyoka nodded. "You're an African, the same as I am. Yet hundreds of Africans starve to death or die of disease every day. They die because most leaders of African countries are petty tyrants who don't give a damn about their people. You know that as well as I do, Mafuta. And we don't give a damn either. If we did, we wouldn't be here. If we don't care about the lives of other Africans, why should we worry about the British?"

"You're both mercenaries," Hizam commented with disgust. "Captain Nyoka is simply more honest and has more stomach for his profession. No matter. This time you serve a higher purpose by helping to humiliate and cripple the enemies of Libya."

"Wonderful," Nyoka muttered sourly. "Just make sure I get paid and I'll help you blow up all of London if you want."

"Don't worry, Captain," Hizam assured him. "You'll be taken care of."

Hizam's features did not betray his amusement. Nyoka and Mafuta did not realize they would not survive to return to Africa. They did not appreciate the importance of world opinion or how it affects international relations.

To simply blow up the embassy and kill a couple hundred English would only serve to enrage world opinion against the puppet government of Mardaraja. This would naturally lead to a United Nations investigation that would probably reveal that the tiny African nation was owned and operated by Colonel Khaddafi.

Major Hizam would never have conducted a mission that might embarrass his beloved leader. He considered himself to be a patriotic Libyan. Hizam was willing to sacrifice his life—or anyone else's—for Khaddafi, Libya and Allah...in that order.

The other Libyans under Hizam's command were also Khaddafi loyalists and suicidal fanatics. They had willingly accepted the mission, fully aware they would not return to their homeland alive.

The bomb would be detonated while everyone, Mardarajan as well as Libyan, was inside the embassy. The explosion would destroy the building and everyone in it. The destruction would certainly spread for at least two blocks. Most, if not all, of the soldiers and police outside the embassy would be killed. Dozens of other British would also be injured by the blast and flying debris. Terrible death and destruction would fall upon London like a flaming sword in the vengeful hands of Allah.

The world would be shocked by the incident. President Skrubu would accuse the British government of ordering the Mardarajan embassy to be blown to bits. He would declare this to be an act of war against Mardaraja—a tiny Third World nation incapable of retaliation against the British giant.

Of course, the United Kingdom would deny this, but England would not be able to prove what actually happened. Few would believe the explosion was detonated by suicidal zealots within the embassy. Naturally, the United Nations would conduct an investigation. The same United Nations that condemned Britain's actions in the Falkland Islands and the U.S. invasion of Grenada, yet never criticized the Soviets' activity in Afghanistan or Poland. The same United Nations that is largely composed of Communist countries and Third World nations—few of which have any fondness for the United Kingdom.

Great Britain would be criticized and condemned by the rest of the world. Her humiliation and loss of face would cripple her diplomatic and political strength. Major Hizam and the other Libyan fanatics regarded this goal as a victory worth dying for.

Hizam was actually eager to sacrifice himself for the cause. He would die a martyr and his soul would join Allah in Paradise. However, Hizam had to wait until the British had ample time to announce that diplomatic relations with Mardaraja had been severed. The international press coverage of the incident promised that this would be a top news item throughout the world.

Twenty-four hours should be enough time, Hizam thought with expectation. Twenty-four hours until we write a new chapter of history. A chapter to be written in blood.

13

Colonel Katzenelenbogen, David McCarter and Gary Manning grimly watched the screen of a television set hooked up to a videotape recorder. They were seated in Major Hillerman's den. The feature on the telly was a rerun of Assistant Secretary Heywood's arrival at the Mardarajan embassy.

"Look at that," Katz said, his eyes fixed on the screen. "Notice how the so-called protesters outside the embassy began to back away when Ambassador Mafuta headed for the building."

"Yeah," Manning added. "They're all off the street before the first shot is fired. Those protesters were planted there as an excuse for the shooting."

"And to be sure the press would be on hand," McCarter stated. "All part of a bloody setup from the beginning."

"That's the way Special Military Intelligence sees it," Hillerman declared as he limped to the television and shut off the VCR. "In fact, the SIS believes there might be a connection with Admiral Harker's assassination as well. Everyone thought it was a random act by a team of Scottish terrorists, but he was murdered after he left the ambassadors' ball at the Banqueting House. An SIS chap on duty that night recalls that Harker was asking a lot of questions about the Mardarajan embassy."

"Too bad more people weren't suspicious." Mc-

Carter sighed. "The admiral must have been a good intel man."

"I knew Harker," Hillerman nodded. "He was very good at spotting threats to national security. A very good man and a very good friend."

"You said you have blueprints of the embassy?" Gary Manning inquired.

"Yes," Hillerman replied, handing the Canadian a thin manila folder. "There's also a blowup of a photograph of the bloke we think is in charge of the terrorists inside the embassy."

Katz examined the photo while Manning looked over the blueprints. The Israeli grunted and nodded when he recognized the face in the picture.

"Abdul Hizam," he declared. "A Khaddafi loyalist and total fanatic. Probably Khaddafi's top coordinator of terrorist activity operating in the Middle East and Northern Africa."

"Jesus," Manning remarked. Katz's memory never failed to amaze the Canadian. "You're like a computer when it comes to international terrorists."

"Well, Hizam's file makes quite an impression," the Israeli replied. "He's had a rather busy career recruiting, training and organizing terrorist activity. For a while he was suspected of being connected with the Muslim extremist group that assassinated President Sadat in Egypt."

"Mr. Torberg is correct," Hillerman began, using Katz's cover name. "Hizam is a fanatic, but a professional. Close to genius IQ and a linguist who speaks Arabic, French, English and Swahili fluently. Hizam is a master manipulator and he spent considerable time in the Congo region, including the area that recently became Mardaraja."

"So Khaddafi has been playing power games in Africa,'' McCarter mused. "Everything's beginning to make sense now."

"Glad you think so." Hillerman sighed. "Oh, SMI and SIS computer checks were unable to identify any of the other terrorists at the embassy, except for one of the black Africans who's been a mercenary for about twenty years. Chap has popped up all over Africa using different names each time. Appears to be totally apolitical and amoral."

"Twenty years of experience makes him a professional," Katz commented. "And we'd better assume the rest of the terrorists are also well trained."

"They're certainly well armed," McCarter said, lighting a Player's cigarette. "Khaddafi must have supplied them with their arsenal. That bastard must be behind this whole business."

"What does Khaddafi hope to accomplish by a stunt like this?" Gary Manning wondered aloud. "I never figured the colonel was anything but just plain nuts, but I can't see any logical motive for this embassy terrorism."

"Perhaps this is Khaddafi's way of getting revenge," Katz suggested as he tugged at the glove covering his prosthetic right hand.

"Revenge?" Hillerman frowned. "Libyans have committed acts of terrorism in England before, but we've never done the same in Khaddafi's country. What does he want revenge for?"

"Less than a month after the Libyan embassy incident in London," Katz began, "there was an unsuccessful attempt to assassinate Colonel Khaddafi in Tripoli."

"The British government wasn't involved in that," Hillerman replied.

"If it was involved," Manning asked dryly, "would you admit it?"

"Probably not," the SMI officer said with a shrug. "But we *were not* involved."

"But Khaddafi might *think* we were," McCarter stated. "It doesn't matter who was really responsible for the attempt on Khaddafi's life. If he *believes* Britain tried to assassinate him, this Mardaraja embassy mess might be his idea of teaching us a lesson."

"There is another possibility," Katz declared. "Khaddafi might not be responsible for the terrorists at the Mardarajan embassy."

"Good God." Hillerman rolled his eyes at the ceiling. "All the evidence points at Khaddafi."

"Let me explain," Katz urged. "We can safely assume that Mardaraja is a puppet of Colonel Khaddafi that he pretty well owns and controls. Now, I doubt that he went to all the expense and effort of creating an entire new country simply to carry out a single act of terrorism."

"The Soviet Union has been gradually taking over African countries one after the other," Manning remarked. "Perhaps Khaddafi is helping Moscow seize control of the Congo region."

"Khaddafi isn't on such good terms with the Soviets these days," Katz replied. "He still owes Moscow about two billion dollars for technology and weaponry sold in the past. The Russians want their money, but Khaddafi feels they owe him a few favors—and probably a discount or two—for services already rendered."

"I remember that now," Hillerman remarked. "Khaddafi even tried to patch up things with the Americans. The United States broke off diplomatic relations and trade with Libya years ago. Khaddafi wanted to start selling oil to the Yanks again, but the Americans weren't interested."

"Khaddafi might be Mr. Personality in Libya, but he

isn't very popular anywhere else," Katz stated. "Most of the other Arab leaders aren't too fond of him. President Sadat once called Khaddafi a vicious criminal possessed by a demon and President Numeiry of Sudan said Khaddafi had a split personality—and both are evil. Even the PLO once referred to him as a maniac. Since Khaddafi doesn't have many allies these days, perhaps he decided to try to create his own in the Congo."

"That would explain why Hizam was in the Congo region before Mardaraja became a nation," McCarter agreed. "And Hizam is an A-number-one fanatic. That means he probably has a rat's maze of mental conditions for a mind."

"I never saw a terrorist who wasn't crazy," Manning said. "Paranoia, schizophrenia, delusions of grandeur and God knows what else. I see what you guys mean now. Hizam and the other Khaddafi loyalists may have taken it upon themselves to carry out this terrorism against England."

"Exactly," Katz confirmed. "If that's the case, Hizam may have actually convinced himself that Khaddafi ordered him on a mission that the colonel knows nothing about."

"And if Hizam was the middle man between Skrubu and Khaddafi," Manning added, "both Mardaraja and Libya might not realize what is really going on."

"Neither do we," McCarter said, crushing out his cigarette in an ashtray. "We've come up with some interesting theories, but we'll probably never know all the facts behind this business. It doesn't really matter anyway. All we have to take care of are the terrorists in the embassy."

"But how are you going to get into the embassy?" Hillerman inquired.

"I've looked over these blueprints," Manning replied. "And I haven't found a weakness that can help us. I had hoped the sewer system might be a way to get under the building so we could break through to the basement, but the pipes are too narrow. A skinny rat might make it, but not a person. The windows would be the easiest way to enter—if the place wasn't surrounded by soldiers and cops."

"I've got an idea how we might be able to get past the security net to the embassy," McCarter announced. "Getting inside will be easy then."

"There are newspaper reporters and television cameras all over the place," Manning reminded him. "Every move we make will be televised all over the world."

"I know," McCarter assured him. "I've got an idea about that too."

"I hate your ideas," the Canadian muttered. "But let's hear it anyway."

"This isn't the place to discuss the fine points of our plan," Katz told his partners. "No offense, Major, but we have our security to consider."

"Of course," Hillerman agreed. "The less I know the better. I just hope you chaps bear in mind you'll be taking on an entire building full of terrorists. The odds will be almost ten to one, you know."

"We're aware of that, Major," Katz replied.

"And you've considered the fact that even if you get inside the embassy and manage to defeat the terrorists," Hillerman continued, "you'll still have to leave the building without falling into the hands of the soldiers and the police outside?"

"Well, David—" Manning turned to the British member of Phoenix Force "—have you included that in your plan?"

"I didn't say it was perfect," McCarter said with a shrug. "But I'm sure we'll come up with something."

"Oh, my God," the Canadian groaned, shaking his head with despair.

14

The Lynx HAS-2 helicopter sailed through the late morning sky like a monstrous dragonfly. Two Africans, stationed on the roof of the Mardarajan embassy watched the chopper. One terrorist opened his tweed jacket to take a walkie-talkie from his belt while the other sentry raised his field glasses to get a better look at the aircraft.

"Relax, N'Cromo," the man with the binoculars told his partner. "It's just the BBC helicopter again. We're being filmed for television. Want to wave at the camera?"

"I don't like this, Tanga," N'Cromo said gruffly. "The military is probably checking all the film the TV people take. They're looking for a weakness in our defenses."

"Let them look," Tanga said with a shrug. "We'll be leaving soon. Diplomatic relations have been severed. Our mission will be over tomorrow morning."

"There could be soldiers in that helicopter," N'Cromo said nervously as he watched the chopper fly a wide orbit around the area.

"It is more than five hundred meters away from us," Tanga said. "It never flies within the restricted area. The soldiers won't let it. The British have to protect our privacy, eh? The helicopter never gets close enough to present a threat and it isn't large enough to carry enough soldiers to attack us anyway."

''They've certainly got plenty of men out there,'' N'Cromo declared, gesturing at the soldiers and police who surrounded the embassy.

''You worry too much,'' Tanga told him. ''Look, the helicopter is going away. Now, will you relax?''

THE BBC CHOPPER HOVERED across Central London. The camera team instructed the pilot to fly over the Thames River in order to film some footage of Westminster Abbey and the Houses of Parliament. The British are quite familiar with these sites, but the BBC would distribute copies of the film to the American press as well. The Yanks always like to have some famous landmarks of London featured in a news story.

Of course, the best known of London's landmarks is probably Big Ben, the 320-foot-high clock tower named after the first commissioner of works, Sir Benjamin Hall. The chopper hovered over the giant clock and slowly moved toward the House of Commons and the House of Lords.

''Good weather for filming,'' Fowley, one of the BBC team, remarked as he aimed his camera at the buildings below. ''No clouds blocking the sun. Clear as a crystal wineglass.''

''Look there,'' Carstairs, the other cameraman, declared. ''The flag is flying from Victoria Tower. That means Parliament is in session. Be sure to film that.''

''Doesn't mean they're meeting to discuss the embassy rot,'' Fowley said. ''Could be another M.P. has been caught mucking about in things he shouldn't.''

''Film the flag anyway,'' Carstairs insisted. ''Let the bloody writers worry about the rest of the story.''

''If you chaps 'ave enough pictures—'' Finch, the pilot, shouted at the pair to be heard above the twin

Rolls-Royce Gem 10001 turbines ''—can we get back to base?''

''You're not running out of petrol, are you?'' Carstairs asked fearfully. He had heard horror stories about helicopter crashes. Bloody things burst into flames like a Molotov cocktail.

''No,'' Finch replied. ''I'm just afraid you blokes might want me to fly up to Northern Ireland to film the bleedin' bomb sites at Belfast next.''

''Well, you needn't fret,'' Fowley scoffed. ''Not good for your blood pressure anyway, don't you know.''

''Unless you ninnies want to swing by Buckingham Palace to ask the Queen if'n she'd care to 'ave us for tea,'' Finch said dryly, ''I'm going to land this bird and take a break.''

''You're tired already?'' Carstairs snorted. ''All you've had to do is fly this chopper about. We haven't even been gone from the base for a full hour yet.''

''You two 'ave made me hover in a fixed position every time you wanted to play with your ruddy cameras,'' the pilot complained. ''That's no bloody picnic. I've gotta use the cyclic to maintain position, watch the altitude with the collective and work the rudders all at the same time. Makin' a turn ain't easy either. If I make a mistake, we might go sailin' into one of them buildin's.''

''All right.'' Carstairs sighed. ''We've finished all the shooting for a while anyway.''

''Ducky,'' Finch muttered sourly.

The Hartnett Insurance Company had agreed to lease its rooftop helicopter pad to the British Broadcasting Corporation. Since the Hartnett building is located on Charterhouse Street, it was considerably closer to the Mardarajan embassy than BBC headquarters. Finch sighed with relief when he saw the Hartnett building.

"Land this bloody thing and get meself a pint," he vowed under his breath.

The chopper hovered over the building. The rooftop looked a bit cluttered from the air. There was a fuel tank positioned near the helicopter pad as well as a storage shed and a watchman's shack. So long as they kept the pad clear, Finch did not care if they decided to breed elephants on the roof. The pilot applied gradual downward pressure to the collective, and the chopper slowly descended. When the wheels touched the pad, Finch shoved the collective down all the way.

"Safe and sound, mates," he announced.

"There should be someone here to meet us," Carstairs complained, glancing about at the deserted roof. "There isn't even a watchman on duty. We need to get this film over to BBC in a hurry, you know."

"Didn't you radio ahead and tell them to expect us?" Fowley asked Finch.

"'Course I did," the pilot said gruffly. "You was with me when I contacted 'em. 'ell, mate, they give me permission to land. The 'igh mandarins knew we was comin', but I reckon they didn't feel you blokes deserved a bleedin' brass band to greet you."

"Well," Carstairs said stiffly, "let's see if anyone inside remembers who we are."

The cameraman emerged from the chopper and headed for a door on the roof while Finch wrote in his log book. Carstairs and Fowley moved to the door casing. They stopped abruptly, startled by what they saw.

A heavy steel bolt had been welded across the door. It was impossible for anyone to get out or enter.

"Why would anyone do this?" Fowley asked, although he did not expect an answer.

"I don't know what's going on," Carstairs replied

tensely. "But I think we'd better get the hell out of here."

Without warning, the door to the storage shed burst open. Three ominous figures rushed forward. Checkered *keffiyeh* were draped over their heads. Ski masks covered their faces. They wore loose-fitting gray coveralls, gloves and black paratrooper boots. Two men carried Uzi submachine guns. The third held an M-16 assault rifle.

"Good God!" Carstairs exclaimed. He thrust his hands overhead, dropping a clipboard.

"Don't move, infidel," the tall, slender man warned, waving his M-16 in a menacing manner. "We will not hesitate to kill if we must do so."

Two more sinister figures, dressed in the same elaborate costume, appeared from the watchman's shack. They aimed Ingram M-10 machine pistols at the helicopter and ordered Finch to get out of the machine.

"What do you want?" Fowley asked. His voice trembled, but he had remained calm enough to put down the TV camera before he raised his hands.

"Don't ask questions, English," a thickly built man, with an Uzi braced across his rigidly held right forearm, warned. "Just do what we tell you and maybe you live. Understand me, English?"

"Move now!" another masked figure snarled as he shoved Finch toward the two cameramen. "Get down on belly. Nose on ground. Do now!"

The trio had no choice. They dropped to the surface of the roof and sprawled in a prone position. One of the captors knelt by Finch and pulled the pilot's arms behind his back. He quickly handcuffed Finch's wrists together and double-locked the manacles.

"If it's the film you want. . . ." Carstairs began.

"Shut mouth, English," the captor snapped as he

cuffed Carstairs next. "We take what we want. Understand me?"

Soon all three captives had been securely handcuffed, gagged and blindfolded. They heard their assailants moving about. Boots crept across the roof. Clothing rustled. Voices communicated softly in different languages. Carstairs recognized a few words in French. Fowley overheard a couple expressions in German and Finch would later claim at least two assailants spoke Spanish.

The five masked figures loaded several large canvas containers onto the Lynx chopper and then climbed inside the machine. The man who took the pilot's seat quickly examined the control panel and nodded to the others to assure them that everything was ready for lift-off.

The masked pilot placed the cyclic control in neutral and slowly raised the collective in a steady, smooth motion. He opened the throttle to increase power as the helicopter rose into the noonday sky.

"There we go, mates," David McCarter announced as he worked the rudder pedals to maintain heading. "How do you like my plan so far?"

"So far we've committed assault with a deadly weapon and stolen a BBC helicopter," Gary Manning replied sourly. "Great start, David."

"Everything is going well so far," Katzenelenbogen assured McCarter. "But this is the easy part. The real challenge has yet to be met."

"So let's go do it," Calvin James urged.

15

"Has something happened we don't know about?" N'Cromo, the apprehensive sentry on the roof of the Mardarajan embassy, remarked as he watched a familiar object hover toward the site.

"What do you mean?" Tanga, his partner, inquired.

"The BBC helicopter is headed back here," N'Cromo explained, pointing at the advancing chopper. "Should I radio Captain Nyoka?"

"No need for that," Tanga replied as he raised his binoculars to get a better look at the aircraft.

"It's coming in closer this time," N'Cromo said nervously, reaching for the walkie-talkie on his belt.

"Will you relax, damn it?" Tanga snapped, trying to train his field glasses on the chopper. "We're not in any danger from...."

Tanga's lower jaw dropped in astonishment when he got a magnified view of the helicopter. A sliding door to the carriage was open. A figure, dressed in dark clothing with a checkered *keffiyeh* over his head, was aiming a rifle at the Mardarajan sentries. Sunlight flashed on the lens of a Bushnell telescopic sight mounted on the rifle.

A narrow tongue of fire sizzled from the muzzle of a sound suppressor attached to the barrel of the Weatherby Vanguard VGX. A big .300 Winchester Magnum projectile rocketed into Tanga's gaping mouth. The high velocity rifle-round knifed through vertebrae and spinal cord. It exploded out the nape of Tanga's neck, creating an exit as big as a silver dollar. Tanga stumbled two steps backward and fell dead.

"Wish I could have gotten some target practice with this rifle," Manning muttered as he worked the bolt of the Weatherby, ejecting the spent cartridge casing and chambering the next round. "That shot was a bit low. I was aiming at his forehead."

"Don't worry," Calvin James remarked. "That dude ain't gettin' up again."

"Cristo," Rafael Encizo rasped as he watched N'Cromo scramble across the roof, walkie-talkie in his fist. "That one has a radio, Gary. If he alerts his comrades we might get shot out of sky before we get a chance to land."

"Nag, nag, nag," Manning growled, peering through the Bushnell scope as he aimed the rifle at N'Cromo.

The terrorist ran for the only cover available, the garret on the roof. N'Cromo raised the walkie-talkie as he galloped for the shelter. He pressed the button to transmit at the very moment a .300 Magnum slug smashed between his shoulder blades. The bullet punched clean through his body and burst from the center of his chest. His backbone broken and his spinal cord cut in two, N'Cromo nosedived to the roof and skidded across the surface until his corpse hit the cornice.

"Good work, Gary," Katzenelenbogen declared. "All right, David. Take us down."

"Here we go," McCarter replied happily, lowering the collective and increasing pressure on the rudders.

He used the cyclic control to hold the airspeed. He did not pull back to slow the chopper until the Lynx had reached the roof and hovered fifty feet above the building. McCarter put the cyclic aft and lowered the collective. The helicopter descended smoothly and gracefully to the roof.

"WHAT THE FUCK is happening up there?" Sergeant Hutton wondered as he and the other SAS troops gazed up at the BBC chopper that had just landed on the roof of the Mardarajan embassy.

"Somebody is attacking the bloody building," Major Geoffrey Simms stated. He peered through a pair of binoculars and watched five bizarre figures emerge from the Lynx.

"Who are they, sir?" Hutton asked. "I take it they're not really the BBC."

"You're really too clever, Sergeant," Simms said with evident sarcasm. "Whoever those blokes are, they're clever devils. They're disguised so well I can't even guess whether they're white, black, Arab or Chinese. They're bundled up so much I can't even describe how they're built. They're not straightening their backs so I can only guess how tall each man is."

"Are they armed?" Hutton wanted to know.

"Oh yes," the major confirmed. "Two men with Uzis, two with Ingram machine pistols and one with an American M-16. From the bulges under their coveralls, I reckon they have other weapons hidden...hullo, what's this?"

Simms watched one of the invaders apply some gray puttylike substance to the door of the garret. The man inserted a pencil detonator and gestured to the others to stand back. The plastic explosive seemed to fizzle and pop like a firecracker, yet the door swung open.

"What is it, sir?" Hutton asked.

"One of those chaps just used some CV-38 to blow open the door," Simms replied. "Couldn't have been easier if he had the ruddy key. Hell of a demo man, whoever he is."

"They're getting inside, sir," the sergeant remarked, stunned by the unexpected event. "What should we do?"

"Well," Simms began, "I suspect those fellows plan to do some damage to the blokes inside the embassy. The only way we could help those poor buggers against this threat would be to enter the embassy to give assistance."

"But we're not authorized to do that, sir," Hutton commented with a wry grin. "That's Mardarajan territory. Not allowed in there, right, sir?"

"President Skrubu said any Englishman caught on Mardarajan soil would be charged with espionage," Simms said with a shrug. "None of us would want to be guilty of that."

"So I guess we'll just have to stand here and watch," the sergeant said, trying not to laugh.

"That's tempting," Simms admitted. "But I'm afraid I'd better radio command headquarters and ask them what the hell we should do now."

"I hope they don't order us to go in and protect those terrorist sods," Hutton muttered.

"There might be too much static on the radio for me to hear their reply," Simms remarked.

"Yes, sir," Hutton agreed happily.

"While I'm on the radio you'd better pass the word to the men that I don't want to hear any of them cheering as if this was a soccer match," Simms instructed. "Bear in mind the press and the bloody television people are still around. Have to present a proper image."

"I suppose so, sir," Hutton said, obviously a bit disappointed.

"Besides," Simms added grimly. "Those five men who just went into that embassy won't be coming out alive, you know."

PHOENIX FORCE ENTERED the building and began to descend a narrow stairwell. Yakov Katzenelenbogen led the way, followed by McCarter and Encizo. James and Manning brought up the rear.

"All right," the Israeli whispered. "Let's get rid of this silly disguise before we roast to death."

They stripped off the *keffiyeh* Arab headdress, ski masks and coveralls. Underneath the bulky garments, each man wore a commando uniform. Knives, ammo pouches and an assortment of grenades hung from their belts. Each man carried an M-17 gas mask in a canvas case on a shoulder sling. Katz, McCarter and Encizo were packing Browning Hi-Power autoloading pistols in shoulder leather. Manning carried a .357 Smith & Wesson revolver and James had a .45 1911A1 Colt.

"You all know what to do," Katz said softly as he checked the foot-long silencer attached to the muzzle of his Uzi. "Try to avoid noisy kills until we can whittle down the odds a bit. Good luck."

"And good hunting," McCarter added with a grin.

16

A pair of Mardarajan terrorists suddenly appeared at the foot of the stairs. They were about to go up to the roof to relieve N'Cromo and Tanga on sentry duty. Instead they found Phoenix Force waiting at the staircase.

The startled terrorists automatically reached for pistols holstered under their tweed jackets. Yakov Katzenelenbogen reacted like the ultimate professional, his reflexes honed by four decades of blood-laced experience. The Israeli colonel fired his Uzi before either African could draw a weapon.

A volley of 9mm projectiles slammed into the terrorists like a backhand from God. One African collapsed, both hands clutching his throat. Two bullets had ripped open the guy's windpipe and severed the carotid artery. Blood squirted between his fingers as he crumpled to the floor.

The other man staggered backward against a doorway. His right biceps had been punctured by a parabellum slug. The high-velocity projectile pierced muscle and buried itself in bone. Katz promptly leaped from the stairs like a battle-scarred lion that was still more than a match for the younger cats in the pride.

The Israeli crashed into the wounded terrorist and both men tumbled across the threshold into the corridor beyond. Katz rammed the muzzle of his Uzi into his opponent's solar plexus. The African doubled up with a gasp and Katz swung his right arm like a club. The edge of his steel hand chopped into the base of the terrorist's neck. The seventh vertebra cracked from the deadly blow. The terrorist dropped to the floor, his neck broken.

But Katz was not alone in the corridor. Two Africans, armed with AK-47 assault rifles, stood at one end of the hallway. Another Mardarajan at the opposite end of the corridor fumbled with a pistol in his belt. All three terrorists were amateurs. They had not expected to stumble upon an unexpected opponent. They needed a split second to cope with their surprise before they reacted to danger.

A split second is enough time to get a man killed when he is pitted against Phoenix Force.

Katz did not hesitate. He immediately trained his Uzi on the two men carrying Kalashnikovs, instinctively striking at the greater threat first. The silenced subgun coughed harshly. One terrorist was hurled backward by the impact of three 9mm slugs in the chest. The other half pivoted and fell to one knee. He dropped his AK-47 to claw at his right side. Two ribs had been shattered by bullets, the splintered tips of bone driven into a lung.

The metallic rasping of another silenced weapon erupted at the same time. David McCarter stood at the doorway, his Ingram M-10 in his fists. Smoke curled from the sound suppressor attached to his box-shaped machine pistol. The third African terrorist lay sprawled on his back, his chest and face ripped to bits by parabellum blasters.

"Hell, Yakov," the Briton said, smiling. "Don't hog all the action, mate."

"I think there'll be enough for everyone," Katz replied as he headed toward the Mardarajan with the punctured lung.

The African glanced up and saw Katz advance. He

tried to call out for help, but pink froth rose up in his throat, nearly choking him. The terrorist made a feeble attempt to grab his Kalashnikov. Katz closed in and kicked the man in the face. The African slumped to the floor unconscious.

A door opened and a Mardarajan peered into the hallway. He had heard strange noises in the corridor, but he was not certain what they meant. A Skorpion machine pistol weaved unsteadily in his trembling hands.

McCarter's M-10 sputtered a quick salvo of destruction. A trio of 119-grain flat-nosed projectiles drilled a grisly pattern in the terrorist's face. The African fell back against the door and slid into a seated position on the floor. Blood trickled from his bullet-torn forehead and a ragged cavity that used to be a nose.

The Briton moved to the wall as he crept toward the room to find out if there were any more enemy gunmen lurking inside. The answer came before he got halfway down the hall. An ebony arm swung around the edge of the doorway and aimed a .38 Colt Positive at McCarter.

The Phoenix Force pro threw himself to the floor and simultaneously triggered a 3-round burst at his opponent. The terrorist's revolver barked. A .38 slug smacked into the wall where McCarter had been a second earlier. However, the Briton's volley of 9mm also failed to claim the intended target. Bullets splintered the doorway, but did not strike flesh.

The terrorist retreated from the doorway. McCarter, however, rolled closer and adopted a prone stance, his Ingram trained on the entrance of the room. The Briton kept his position and waited for his adversary to make the next move.

Timidly, the African peered over the edge of the doorway, the Colt in his fist. He obviously hoped to find McCarter's corpse lying on the floor. For a moment he thought his wish had come true. Then McCarter's M-10 uttered a subdued song of death. A 3-round burst kicked the terrorist back into the room and sent him to oblivion.

"You lose, mate," McCarter rasped as he started to get to his feet.

Thus far only one shot from a weapon without a sound suppressor had been fired, but that was enough to alert the other terrorists of danger. Another door opened and two Africans slipped into the corridor. McCarter's back was turned toward the pair.

Terrorists are not noted for courage. The opportunity to shoot the British warrior in the back was just their cup of tea. The Mardarajan killers raised their Skorpion machine pistols and prepared to blast McCarter.

Then their skulls exploded. Rafael Encizo had seen his British amigo was in trouble. The Cuban promptly aimed his Uzi and opened fire. Parabellum slugs smashed into backs of the terrorists' heads and rearranged their brains. The pair died on their feet and wilted to the floor, unfired Skorpions still in their fists.

Light flashed as polished steel swung toward Encizo's neck. The Cuban raised his Uzi in time to deflect the knife blade with the barrel of the subgun. His assailant's free hand seized the Uzi and tried to wrench the weapon from Encizo's grasp.

The Cuban's opponent was a large black man, much bigger and heavier than Encizo. The African was also a good fifteen years younger than the Bay of Pigs veteran. If they continued to grapple over the weapons, the odds would be in the terrorist's favor.

The African swung his knife again, aiming at the Cuban's throat. Encizo weaved out of the path of the blade, but his fingers slipped from the Uzi. The terrorist abruptly tore the gun from Encizo's hand.

The larger man executed a backhand slash. Encizo jumped away from the knife. His back connected with a wall as the African awkwardly fumbled with the Uzi in his left hand, trying to alter his grip on the weapon in order to use the trigger.

Encizo's leg lashed out in a roundhouse kick. His boot connected with the Uzi, striking it from the Mardarajan's grasp. The terrorist snarled and lunged with the knife. Encizo dodged. The point of the terrorist's weapon stabbed the wall and sunk into plaster.

The Cuban's fingers closed on the haft of the Gerber Mark I on his belt. His arm struck like a scorpion with a five-inch steel stinger. The tip of his fighting dagger pierced the soft skin under the African's jaw. The force of the thrust drove the blade through the guy's tongue, pinning it to the roof of his mouth. Steel punctured bone and lanced the terrorist's brain.

Mardarajan fanatics seemed to be coming out of the woodwork like giant roaches. Gary Manning and Calvin James charged into the corridor as more terrorists emerged from rooms on both sides. Only a few of these were armed with subguns or automatic rifles. Most carried only pistols or knives.

Manning promptly aimed his Ingram M-10 at a Mardarajan armed with an AK-47 who was about to open fire on Katz. The Canadian squeezed the trigger of his machine pistol and pumped three 9mm rounds into the terrorist's neck and skull. The enemy gunman tumbled to the floor, his head swinging, loosely attached to the neck by taut strands of skin and splintered vertebrae.

A primitive battle whoop caused Manning to whirl and confront another aggressor. Two African killers had tried to attack Manning from the rear. The closest was armed with a machete. His comrade had a pistol, but held his fire, allowing the machete-wielding zealot to launch the first charge.

The jungle knife swooped toward Manning's neck as the terrorist tried to decapitate him with a single stroke. The Canadian bent his knees and ducked low. The long blade hissed as it sliced air inches above Manning's head.

The Phoenix Force commando did not let his opponent try another machete stroke. Manning charged into his assailant, ramming the top of his skull into the man's midsection. The terrorist half groaned, half gasped as the unexpected blow drove the breath from his lungs.

Manning shoved hard and lifted the African off the floor. The Canadian suddenly rushed forward and slammed his opponent into the pistol-wielding terrorist. The force of Manning's charge drove both Mardara-jans backward and smashed them against the nearest wall.

The Canadian's left hand snared the first man's wrist above the jungle knife. His right hand thrust the Ingram into the terrorist's chest. He triggered the M-10, blasting a 3-round burst through his opponent's upper torso. The high-velocity projectiles burned a lethal tunnel through the African's heart and punched out his back to drill the second terrorist as well. The two Mardarajan maggots slumped to the floor, astonished to discover they had slid right into the realm of the dead.

"Down, David!" Calvin James shouted at his British colleague.

McCarter did not question the command. He immediately dropped to the floor. A column of 7.62mm bullet holes burst across the plaster of a wall above the Briton's prone form.

The hard-faced terrorist who had tried to waste Mc-Carter snarled with rage when his target suddenly dropped beneath the path of his bullets. The gunman lowered the aim of his Soviet PPSh-41 and prepared to blast the Briton into the hereafter.

James had already raised the black plastic stock of the M-16 to his shoulder. The front sight divided the terrorist's face. The black badass from Chi-town squeezed the trigger. Three 5.56mm slugs obliterated the Mardarajan's features.

One bullet split the guy's cheekbone. Another burst an eyeball and sizzled through the socket into his brain. The third projectile splintered the bridge of his nose and traveled on to cause even more damage to gray matter before it popped an exit wound at the back of his skull. The PPS blaster slipped from lifeless fingers as the terrorist's corpse wilted to the floor.

McCarter glanced at the fallen African and turned to Calvin James. A wide smile split Calvin's ebony features as he held up a fist with the thumb erect. McCarter grinned and returned the thumbs-up gesture.

An unexpected salvo of full-auto rounds slammed into James's M-16. The plastic forestock shattered and bullets whined against the steel barrel. The impact sent the assault rifle hurtling out of the black commando's grasp.

"Shit," James rasped as he quickly whirled and dived to the floor.

A stocky Mardarajan cursed as he fired another burst from his Skorpion machine pistol. Half a dozen 7.65mm projectiles scorched the air above James's hurtling form, but none hit their intended mark. The Phoenix Force champ executed a fast shoulder roll that carried him across the floor and put him less than a yard from the gunman.

The awestruck Mardarajan tried to redirect the aim of his Czech chatter-box. James rocketed up from the floor, his right leg extended in a high side kick. His boot connected with the Skorpion and kicked the weapon back into its owner's face. The terrorist cried out with pain and surprise when the steel frame of the machine pistol smashed into his mouth. The blow shattered two front teeth and the metal sight ripped his upper lip in two.

James pounced on his opponent. His left hand caught the guy's wrist to hold the Skorpion at bay while his right fist drove a *seiken* karate punch to the terrorist's solar plexus. James thrust a heel-of-the-palm stroke under the African's jaw. The Mardarajan buttonman groaned and sagged against the Phoenix Force whirlwind.

"Nguruwembwa!" A terrorist shouted the Swahili version of *Schweinehund* as he aimed a pistol at James.

The Phoenix Force pro quickly seized the Skorpion blaster that was still in the fist of the man he had stunned with a flurry of karate blows. James swung the Czech machine pistol at the dude with the pistol. He pressed his finger on the trigger and fired a full-auto volley. Half a dozen steel-jacketed slugs slammed into the second terrorist. A Yugoslavian handgun fell from the African's fingers as his bullet-shredded corpse slid along the wall and landed on the floor in a trembling heap.

"Thanks, man," James told the dazed Mardarajan as he yanked the Skorpion from the man's grasp.

James suddenly whipped a back fist to the terrorist's right temple. The blow snapped off what little hold on consciousness the African had managed to retain. He dropped like a wet stone and sprawled out on the floor at James's feet.

Two Mardarajan gunmen appeared at the south end of the corridor. Both men were armed with AK-47 assault rifles, but neither lived to fire a single shot. Katz and Encizo instantly hosed the pair with Uzi hellfire.

McCarter took a spent magazine from his M-10 Ingram and prepared to replace it with a fresh mag. Suddenly another rifle-toting terrorist crept into the hall from the north end. The British warrior lunged forward and seized the barrel of the African's AK-47 with both hands. He pulled the startled gunman forward and promptly rammed a knee into the guy's guts. The terrorist folded with a groan.

McCarter grabbed the African by the back of the neck and the seat of the pants. He turned sharply and hauled his opponent headfirst into a wall. The terrorist's skull smashed plaster and struck the wood frame. Blood oozed from the Mardarajan's cracked cranium as he slumped to the floor.

Another terrorist charged into the corridor as Calvin James scooped up an AK-47 from the floor. The gunman aimed his PPS subgun at the black commando. McCarter's right arm became a blur as he rapidly drew his Browning. The Briton snapped off the safety catch and aimed the pistol instinctively, squeezing the trigger in a single, fluid motion.

The Browning roared as the Kalashnikov in James's fist snarled. A 9mm parabellum slug crashed into the side of the terrorist's skull. Four 7.62mm rounds tore into his chest at the same time. The Mardarajan gunman was double-dead before his body hit the floor, the unfired Russian submachine gun locked in a grip frozen by death.

"How many of these scumbags have we killed so far, David?" James inquired as he jogged forward.

"Haven't kept count," McCarter replied, shoving a

32-round magazine into his Ingram machine pistol. "But I don't think we've killed them all yet."

"I think you're right," James muttered as he heard voices shout orders in Swahili amid the slap of boot leather against stone.

James and McCarter moved toward the sound. They slipped around the corner at the end of the hall and discovered a staircase extending to the floor below. Four or five Mardarajan gunmen charged up the steps, weapons held ready.

"Come and get it, you assholes," James snarled as he aimed the Kalashnikov at the group and opened fire.

Two terrorists screamed as bullets smashed into flesh. The bloodied pair tumbled backward into their comrades. The Mardarajans half ran, half stumbled down the stairs, too busy retreating to return fire.

McCarter took an SAS "flash-bang" grenade from his belt and pulled the pin. He tossed the minibomb down the stairwell. The grenade bounced off a riser and landed amid the terrorists at the foot of the stairs.

The concussion grenade exploded, and the blast hurled bodies like rag dolls thrown by a furious child. Blood flowed from nostrils, ears and gaping mouths. McCarter and James galloped down the stairs. The Briton sprayed the mangled terrorists with Ingram rounds to be certain none of them would ever threaten anyone again.

The Phoenix Force pair had descended to another hallway on the second story. The corridor was wide and there appeared to be fewer rooms than they found at the top floor. However, a lone terrorist cautiously poked his head around the corner at the end of the hall.

James snap-aimed his AK-47 and fired a quick burst at the enemy gunman. The terrorist's head disappeared from view. James was not certain whether or not he hit the man.

Suddenly two round objects were tossed around the corner. The serrated metal balls were F-1 hand grenades, the Soviet version of the old World War II Mark 11A1 "pineapple."

"Oh, shit!" James exclaimed as he charged forward and desperately kicked the closest grenade.

The F-1 blaster rocketed down the hallway to the opposite end of the corridor, but James knew he could not reach the other grenade in time. The black man and his British partner dived to the floor beside the pile of dead terrorists at the foot of the stairs. McCarter seized the nearest corpse and dragged it over James's prone figure as a shield.

Then the grenades exploded. The building seemed to quake. Plaster and dust filled the corridor and a section of the ceiling broke loose to crash down on the Phoenix Force pair.

A Libyan terrorist named Mohammed Khatid peeked around the corner. He smiled with satisfaction when he saw the collection of still bodies half buried under rubble. Khatid turned to a pair of Mardarajans under his command.

"Kaziema," he told his African comrades. "Good work. We killed them."

17

"Is it true that my embassy is under attack?" President Skrubu asked in an astonished voice as he sat behind his hand-carved teakwood desk in his office at Ubongo, the capital of Mardaraja. He gripped the telephone receiver so hard his knuckles hurt. "Is it true?"

"It's hardly a state secret, Mr. President," the British PM replied. "The siege is being televised *live* all over the world at this very moment."

"This is an act of war...." Skrubu began.

"It is nothing of the sort," the prime minister assured him. "Whoever attacked the embassy, they are not acting on the orders of my government or any military service of the United Kingdom. I have the home secretary in my office and the director of SIS was here a moment ago. Neither of them has any idea who might be responsible for this incident."

"Do you expect me to believe this?" Skrubu demanded.

"Well, the home secretary suspected the assault on the Mardarajan embassy might be an act of terrorism by Libyan fanatics upset by remarks you made about Colonel Khaddafi," the prime minister replied. "But I told him that you and the colonel are still friends. I assume we can dismiss Libya as a suspect?"

"You're lying to me, you British hag!" Skrubu snapped. "How could these invaders have penetrated the security net surrounding the embassy unless your military allowed them to enter?"

"Whoever these people are," she began, once again ignoring Skrubu's abusive language, "they assaulted a BBC camera crew and stole a helicopter. No one was suspicious of the helicopter until it flew straight for the embassy. A sniper gunned down the two Mardarajans on the roof. Then the aircraft landed and the five mystery men blasted their way into the building."

"*Five* men?" Skrubu inquired. "There are only five of them?"

"That is correct, Mr. President," the prime minister confirmed. "The number of individuals is the only fact we have concerning their identity. All five were wearing masks, gloves and other disguises. The BBC personnel, who were found bound and gagged only a few minutes ago, told us the strangers didn't say much, but they spoke English with a definite accent. They also spoke to each other in at least three languages other than English. So we have not the foggiest notion concerning what nationality these men might be."

"This is an outrage!" Skrubu declared. "Your military isn't even trying to protect my embassy."

"Of course not," the PM admitted. "They can't legally enter the damn building since you severed diplomatic relations."

The prime minister was pacing in front of her desk as she spoke into the telephone. Although noted for her calm dignified manner, the PM was an active woman, charged with enough personal energy to light up London for a week.

The home secretary knew her better than most. He knew that she had a great passion for England and deep concern for the people of Great Britain. She felt joy with England's victories and sorrow for her country's failures.

The prime minister had authorized Operation Nimrod in 1980, eagerly following the advice of the home secretary to allow the SAS to raid the Iranian embassy. Following the success of Nimrod, the prime minister, the home secretary and others at tactical headquarters celebrated by watching a videotape of the rescue operation. The PM had sat cross-legged on the floor, clearly delighted by what she saw.

This same prime minister had been powerless to act against the terrorism at the Libyan embassy in 1984. She had been frustrated by the repetition of such horror during the current Mardarajan embassy incident. Now, five mysterious strangers were trying to make the terrorists pay for this outrage.

The home secretary knew that the prime minister would not publicly praise this unsanctioned assault on the Mardarajan embassy. Indeed, she might be forced to give lip service to those who would surely condemn the actions of the five masked warriors. Yet, the home secretary was certain that, in her heart, the prime minister was cheering for the mystery assault team.

"Am I to understand that you intend to do nothing about this invasion, Madam Prime Minister?" President Skrubu demanded.

"What would you have me do, Mr. President?" she replied, glad that Skrubu could not see the thin smile she was unable to repress. "Order my soldiers to charge into the building so they can be shot down by your people or perhaps by whoever these five lunatics are? Then what, Mr. President? You'll blame the whole business on the British government? I think not, Mr. President."

The door opened and Major Hillerman limped into the office, leaning heavily on his walking stick. The home secretary recognized the officer from Special Military Intelligence and eagerly waved him forward. Hillerman noticed that the prime minister was standing in front of her desk as she spoke in the telephone. She was trying to watch a television set at the same time. Needless to say, the drama at the embassy was on the screen.

"Excuse me, Madam Prime Minister," the home secretary began. "This is Major Hillerman from SMI. I believe he has some news for you concerning the Mardarajan embassy."

"President Skrubu is on the line," she answered. "Perhaps the major will be good enough to talk to him as he makes this report so the president can hear all the details first hand."

"Of course," Hillerman agreed, taking the telephone receiver from the PM. "Are you there, Skrubu?"

"That's *President* Skrubu," the voice replied from the earpiece.

"I'm a soldier, not a diplomat, Skrubu," Hillerman said gruffly. "I don't have to kiss your arse. Now, do you want to hear what SMI has on this business or not?"

"I'm listening," Skrubu answered stiffly.

"So am I, Major," the PM assured him as she perched on the edge of her desk.

"Well," the major began, "SMI believes the chaps who have laid siege to the embassy are probably a group of professional mercenaries. They're armed with weapons that are available through markets, legal and otherwise, in Western Europe and the United States. We suspect that the mercenaries are most probably Western Europeans of mixed nationalities. Germans and French, perhaps. Might be one or two former Franco fascists in the group. Some of them joined the French Foreign Legion, you know. This would explain the different languages they used according to those BBC chaps."

"But who sent these hired killers to attack my embassy?" Skrubu demanded.

"Haven't the foggiest, old boy," Hillerman replied

cheerfully. "Probably some rich old patriot who doesn't approve of you bastards mucking about shooting British citizens. At any rate, an attack by a group of mercenaries is not a matter of international law unless the blokes were hired by a particular government. Since that hasn't happened in this case, I'd say you have a private little war going on at your precious embassy. All we Britons can do is stand by and watch."

"I want to speak to the prime minister," Skrubu told him.

Hillerman handed the telephone to the PM. Her eyes were locked on the television screen. A long-range camera shot of the Mardarajan embassy showed figures darting about at the windows. The place was obviously in turmoil. The terrorists were getting a dose of their own violent medicine and they did not seem to like it.

"Madam Prime Minister?" Skrubu asked sharply.

"Yes, Mr. President," she replied, shifting a buttock on the edge of her desk. Her skirt rode up above a knee. Hillerman smiled. He had always admired the PM and he liked her legs too.

"Are you going to simply allow these mercenaries to slaughter Mardarajan diplomats and walk away scot-free?" Skrubu asked.

"That will depend," the prime minister answered.

"Depend on what?" Skrubu wanted to know.

"Whether or not the mercenaries have diplomatic immunity, of course," she replied dryly.

President Skrubu abruptly hung up.

"Bravo, Madam Prime Minister," Hillerman said sincerely.

"Unfortunately," she began, "if those five mercenaries or whatever they are manage to get out of the embassy alive, the soldiers and the police will have to apprehend them."

"I'm afraid that's true," the home secretary added with a sigh. "Can't have chaps stealing BBC helicopters and running about with automatic weapons to play vigilante... even when you rather admire what they're trying to do."

"I suppose not," Hillerman replied. "Pity really. They're really doing a bloody great job in a way."

"Not to worry, Major," the PM stated. "Those fellows will have to stand trial, of course, but I'm certain no British court will sentence them to prison. They'll simply be deported to whatever country they came from. Probably write a book about their adventure and it will become a best-seller. Especially here in England."

"Perhaps," the home secretary said grimly. "But it'll be a miracle if any of them survive."

"Miracles happen from time to time, sir," Hillerman said. "I suppose I'd best get back to my post now. May I say it's been a pleasure to watch you in action, Madam Prime Minister."

Hillerman's eyes had shifted to the PM's legs once more. She hastily tugged at her skirt and climbed down from the desk.

"Uh...thank you, Major," she said formally. "That will be all."

Yet there was a twinkle in her eye. The prime minister was, after all, a woman.

Major Hillerman limped from the PM's office. His professional poker face concealed a dozen troubled thoughts. A small army of terrorists was inside the embassy. McCarter and his four friends would almost certainly be killed. If they survived, their identities would become public knowledge and whatever sort of top-secret commando unit they worked for would be ruined forever. Unless they could become invisible at will,

Hillerman did not see any way those five brave warriors would be able to leave the embassy without falling into the hands of the SAS or the Royal Marines.

If they were identified, the link between Hillerman and McCarter from their old SAS days would also put the major under suspicion. His involvement would incorrectly place the blame on the SMI and thus on the British government as well. This would be a terrible scandal and an embarrassment for the entire nation. It would destroy the very purpose for bringing in McCarter's group in the first place.

And England would not suffer alone. Whoever the commandos were, they obviously had connections with the American government. The Yanks would also be in for a nasty scandal. In fact, the entire free world would suffer because it would lose a very effective and dedicated force in the battle against terrorism, tyranny and savagery.

"Oh, Christ," Hillerman whispered under his breath. "I hope those chaps have one hell of a good trick or two up their sleeves."

ON THE OPPOSITE SIDE of the ocean, yet another world leader was concerned about the siege on the Mardarajan embassy. The President of the United States had heard that five mysterious warriors had assaulted the building. He immediately hurried to a secure chamber where he pushed out a coded telephone number on a line equipped with a sophisticated scrambling device. Both the code and the scrambler were changed once a week to be certain the line could not be tapped—even by the CIA.

"Yes, Mr. President," Hal Brognola's voice came over the line.

"You've been expecting me to call?" the President asked.

"I'm not really surprised, sir," Brognola admitted.

"Will you please tell me where Phoenix Force is at this very moment?" the President inquired.

"I'm not absolutely certain, Mr. President."

"Have you heard what's happening in London right now?"

"I have the TV on, sir," Brognola answered with a sigh.

"And you're still not sure where they are?"

"I . . . have a pretty good idea where they might be."

"If Phoenix Force gets back from London alive," the President began tensely, "and they don't burn their cover—and I don't see how they'll do either one of those miracles, let alone both—we're going to have to have another talk, Hal."

"Uh-huh," the Stony Man commander grunted. "Right now, I'm more concerned about the lives of five good men, Mr. President."

"There's more at stake here than five lives and you know it, Hal."

"Yeah," Brognola agreed wearily, "I know."

"I'll talk to you later," the President said. "After I've had some aspirin."

"Yes, sir," Brognola replied.

Both men hung up. Brognola jammed a cigar in the corner of his mouth and bit down on it hard.

"Shit," he muttered. "They did it again."

18

Mohammed Khatid and the more Mardarajan gunmen cautiously approached the pile of rubble. They were ninety-eight percent certain that Calvin James and David McCarter had been killed by the grenade blast, but they wanted to be absolutely sure.

"They couldn't have lived through that," one of the Africans remarked, but the AK-47 quivering in his unsteady grasp belied his confidence.

"We'll make certain of that by shooting them both in the head," Khatid replied. "But don't worry. They're certainly badly injured and unable to fight."

The two Africans made no comment, but they noticed that Khatid had elected to stay behind them.

They reached the mound of plaster-covered bodies. Most of these were the corpses of slain terrorists, although the bodies of McCarter and James also appeared to be devoid of life. One of the Mardarajans leaned forward and used the barrel of his Kalashnikov to brush some chunks of plaster from a still figure. It was a dead African, draped over Calvin James.

The terrorist used the stock of his AK-47 as a lever and pried the corpse off the black commando's inert form. James's right arm suddenly rose, the Government Issue Army Colt in his fist. The big gun bellowed. A .45 slug smashed the terrorist's face into crimson pulp.

James thrust a leg high and kicked the dead man

backward into Khatid. The corpse hit the Libyan's fore-arm, knocking the Makarov from his grasp. The second Mardarajan gunman aimed his Kalashnikov at James, but the Phoenix Force fighter's pistol snarled once more.

The African screamed as he stumbled into a wall and dropped his rifle. The terrorist's left elbow had been shattered by a 230-grain solid-ball projectile. His right hand clutched his bullet-crushed limb as he tried to decide whether to reach for his side arm, surrender or allow himself to pass out.

James began to rise up from the rubble, but Khatid rushed forward and lashed out a boot. The kick struck James's hand and sent the Colt flying. Khatid had been well trained. His leg executed a fast crescent kick. The edge of his foot slammed into the black man's face.

James tumbled backward and rolled on his neck and shoulders. He completed the back roll and sprang to his feet. The Phoenix Force pro assumed a T-*dachi* stance, one arm extended, the other held close to his body.

"Try that again, you goddamn camel-fucker," James shouted, hoping to enrage Khatid. An angry man tends to make angry mistakes.

Khatid smiled thinly and replied to the challenge with a curt nod. The Libyan realized what James had tried to do by the insult. He adopted a karate cat stance and shuffled toward the black man.

Khatid's hands flashed in a quick feint as he snapped a toe kick at James's crotch. The black man's fist shot out and pumped a pistonlike *seiken* punch to the ter-rorist's shin. Khatid grunted with pain and swung both hands at James's head, hoping to catch it with a double palm-heel stroke to both temples.

James raised both forearms to block the attack. He quickly hooked a left fist to Khatid's jaw, followed by a right cross. The Libyan staggered two steps backward. James immediately canted his body and thrust a tae kwon-do kick to his opponent's face.

Khatid fell against a wall, blood gushing from his crushed nose. James rushed forward and slashed a cross-body *shuto* stroke at the Libyan. The side of his hand struck his opponent's throat hard. The deadly blow smashed Khatid's windpipe and crushed the thyroid cartilage. The Libyan clasped both hands to his wrecked throat and fell to the floor in a dying lump.

The wounded Mardarajan was horrified. The tall black stranger had just killed Lieutenant Khatid with his bare hands. The African desperately clawed at the button-flap holster on his hip.

"Hey, mate!" a voice called out.

The Mardarajan half-turned to face the speaker. A handful of plaster dust flew into his open mouth and eyes. The terrorist stumbled backward, pawing at his face with his right hand.

David McCarter dashed forward and thrust a fist into the side of his opponent's head. A bent knuckle struck the terrorist's sphenoid. The thin bone caved in, driving broken shards into the African's brain.

The Mardarajan dropped lifeless to the floor. McCarter fell to one knee beside the corpse, shaking his head to clear it. James hurried to his partner's side.

"Take it easy, man," James urged as he examined a blood-laced cut at McCarter's hairline.

"I'm all right, Calvin," the Briton assured him.

"I'm the medic, damn it," James snapped. "I'll tell you if you're okay or not. You could have a concussion or even a fractured skull."

"You'll have to x-ray me later," McCarter said gruffly. "Right now we need Phoenix Force at full strength and that means I've got to stay on my feet."

"Let's see if I can't help you do that," James said as he hauled the Briton upright. "I've got some Benzedrine in my bag. That ought to keep you going for a while. I just hope you don't drop dead when it wears off."

"Just give me one tablet," McCarter told him. "I don't want to be turned into a bloody drug addict."

"One little pep pill won't turn you into a junkie," James stated as he reached for the medic kit at the small of his back. "It's when you start getting your kicks by popping bennies that you've got a problem. You already get your jollies with these nutty missions, so you're already sick anyway."

"Maybe." The Briton grinned. "But I love it, don't you know."

"Yeah," James said. He glanced at the Mardarajan McCarter had killed with a single blow. "What kind of punch did you use on that dude, David?"

"A Chinese kung fu technique," McCarter replied with a wolfish smile. "Called a *feng-yen* stroke. Bit of irony in that."

"How's that?" the black man inquired.

"The stroke is also called the 'eye of the Phoenix,'" McCarter explained.

An eruption of full-auto fire suddenly echoed through the building. McCarter instinctively drew his Browning pistol as James once again scooped up a Kalashnikov from a slain terrorist. Two Mardarajan gunmen plunged into the corridor at the opposite end of the hall.

The Phoenix Force pair held their fire. The terrorists had stumbled backward and collapsed to the floor, their shirts bloodied and torn by bullets. The snout of an Uzi submachine gun poked around the edge of the corner. Katzenelenbogen stepped into view, his Israeli blast-machine cradled against his prosthetic right arm, muzzle aimed at the ceiling.

"We wondered what happened to you two," the Phoenix Force commander commented dryly. He glanced at the corpses that littered the hallway. "Glad to see you've managed to stay busy."

Rafael Encizo and Gary Manning emerged behind the Israeli colonel. McCarter and James were relieved to see all three of their partners had survived the gun battle without a scratch.

"How'd you dudes get down here?" James inquired.

"Found another flight of stairs," Encizo replied. "Pretty easy because you two had drawn most of the fire already."

"Doesn't look like there were nearly as many terrorists on this floor as we encountered upstairs," Gary Manning remarked as he unslung a field pack from his back.

"I suspect most of them have fled to the first story," Katz stated. "Terrorists aren't professional soldiers. They tend to run from a face-to-face fight."

"Yeah," James commented, checking the magazine of his confiscated AK-47 to be certain of his ammo supply. "But I figure we've already killed more than half of the bastards."

"Don't forget we're dealing with fanatics," Encizo warned. "Most of them have a yellow streak down their backs, but that doesn't mean they won't fight like lunatics when they're cornered. We've got them boxed into the same area downstairs. That means they can either go outside and surrender to the soldiers or they can make one last stand against us."

"Pretty unlikely they'll surrender," Katz replied. "Not with Abdul Hizam in charge of the operation. He'd sooner blow this building to hell and all us with it."

"We'd better get to our mission before he does exactly that," McCarter remarked.

"Right," the Israeli agreed. "Gary, you'd better set up those canisters now."

"I thought you wanted me to do that after we finished with the terrorists," the Canadian demolitions expert said with a frown.

"That was the original plan." Yakov nodded. "But we can expect to encounter some booby traps and such downstairs. There are bound to be more explosions. If the soldiers outside decide that the violence inside the embassy is apt to spread to threaten British citizens, they may raid the place. Besides, somebody might just put a bullet in Hizam's head if the other terrorists decide to surrender. Either way we'd need those canisters in place with the radio detonators ready."

"Are you sure that equipment will work?" Encizo inquired, turning to Manning. "Those radio detonators can be tricky."

"The detonators aren't the problem," Manning assured him. "I brought them from the States. I just hope the canisters work."

"Don't worry," McCarter said. "You can trust equipment when you buy it from Felix Holmes. All the guns and grenades have worked fine, haven't they?"

"I hope we can trust Holmes to carry out the rest of his bargain," Encizo said dryly. "The guy is only interested in money."

"He hasn't been paid for that part yet," McCarter said with a shrug. "He'll be ready when we are."

"If he isn't," the Cuban remarked grimly, "we'll be in one hell of a mess."

"This isn't the time for debate," Katz insisted. "Calvin, go with Gary. He'll need somebody to watch his back while he sets the charges."

"Okay, Yakov," James agreed glumly. He would rather join the others for the main assault, but he didn't argue with Katz's decision.

"Bear in mind that timing is crucial for the total success of this mission," Katz told his men. "And time is running out."

19

Jino slipped on the leopard-skin gauntlets. He smiled with his hideous filed teeth as he examined the curved claws that jutted above the knuckles of his fist. The African fanatic tightened the leather straps to hold the gauntlets in place.

"What the hell are you wearing those things for?" Captain Nyoka demanded when he saw Jino had donned the leopard claws.

"I have armed myself to fight the invaders, of course," Jino replied simply.

"Take those pussycat paws off and get your gun, damn it," Nyoka snapped. "The enemy is obviously armed with submachine guns and grenades. You intend to fight them with a pair of leopard claws? You think your cat god is going to protect you from bullets and shrapnel?"

"You do not understand Paka Munga," Jino told him with the smugness of a religious zealot, certain he knew the only true path to Heaven. "You do not understand anything. This will be our final battle, Captain. The time has come for us to die."

"Die," the mercenary whispered as the awful truth of Jino's statement struck home.

The embassy was surrounded by British soldiers and police. An attack force was already inside the building, fighting its way down to the bottom level. Jino was right. It was time to die.

"This will be my last opportunity to kill," Jino continued. "I want to do it in the manner of the leopard, the messenger of Paka Munga on earth. My god will be pleased. He will welcome me gladly into the next world where the souls of my victims wait to serve me for the rest of eternity."

"I'm glad you're looking forward to it," Nyoka muttered sourly.

The mercenary left Jino in the library. He did not want to be in the same room with the fanatic. Jino wanted to kill one last victim and he was crazy enough to attack anyone with his leopard claws just to please Paka Munga.

Nyoka headed for Ambassador Mafuta's office. The ambassador and Major Hizam were inside. So were three other Libyan terrorists, including Sergeant-Major Waddid, the unit demolitions expert. Waddid had assembled the bomb when they arrived at the embassy. Nyoka had never seen Waddid stray from his explosives until now. The sergeant-major had formerly guarded the bomb as a mother ostrich protects her nest.

However, what truly startled and amazed the mercenary was the fact that all four Libyans had laid down their weapons. Hizam and his men had placed prayer rugs on the floor. The Libyans knelt on the rugs, facing east toward Mecca as they prayed. They sang softly as they bowed their heads to the floor.

"Asha-du Allah ilaha illa Allah," they chanted. "I witness that there is no God but Allah."

"Has everyone gone mad?" Nyoka demanded.

The Libyans ignored him.

"They're singing their death song," Ambassador Mafuta explained as he cowered behind his desk, wringing his hands in despair.

"I know what they're doing, damn it," Nyoka

snapped. "These bastards got us into this mess and now they want us to die with them because they don't have enough guts to put up a goddamn fight...."

Nyoka aimed his AK-47 at the Libyans, but they continued to ignore him. Furious, the mercenary marched into the room and savagely kicked Hizam in the ribs. The major cried out as he tumbled across the floor.

The other Libyans immediately leaped to their feet and prepared to launch themselves at the mercenary. Nyoka pointed his Kalashnikov at the terrorists. They held back, glaring at the African gunman.

An explosion roared from the hallway. To Nyoka's astonishment, the Libyans began to cheer. Their pleasure was short-lived, however, when they heard the metallic rattle of full-auto weapons and screams of agonized victims in the corridor.

"What do you idiots look so disappointed for?" Nyoka demanded. "Because you weren't blown to bits by the explosion...."

"That's correct, Nyoka," Major Hizam replied as he rose to his feet. "Sergeant Major Waddid activated the timer to the detonator of the bomb."

"I set it for five minutes to allow us ample time to pray," Waddid declared proudly.

"You bloody lunatic!" Nyoka screamed as he triggered his Kalashnikov.

A trio of 7.62mm rounds ripped into Waddid's upper torso. The force of the bullets kicked his body backward into a bookcase. The Libyan smashed the glass pane of the cabinet door. Waddid's corpse dragged the furniture and tipped it over as he fell to the floor. Half a dozen books and numerous chunks of broken glass showered the dead sergeant's prone form.

"My God," Ambassador Mafuta gasped in horror.

Hizam and the other two Libyans lunged at Nyoka. A

Khaddafi loyalist grabbed the barrel of the mercenary's AK-47. Nyoka moved with the pull and jammed the muzzle of his weapon into the man's chest. He fired two rounds straight through the Arab's chest. The Libyan held onto the rifle as he fell backward and succeeded in yanking it from Nyoka's hands. The terrorist crashed to a prayer rug where he died with the Kalashnikov still in his fists.

Nyoka swung a fist into the other Libyan trooper's face. Hizam closed in and hooked a heel of the palm stroke to the side of the merc's head. Nyoka doubled up with a groan and Hizam chopped a *shuto* stroke to his opponent's neck muscle.

The word "Nyoka" means snake in Swahili. The mercenary lived up to his name. His right hand snatched a bayonet from an ankle sheath and shot out like a striking serpent. Abdul Hizam screamed as six inches of sharp steel plunged into his stomach.

The Libyan major stumbled into the desk, both hands clutching the terrible puncture wound in his belly. Hizam gazed up at Ambassador Mafuta, his eyes filled with pain and pleading for help. He raised a hand, blood dripping from his palm. His mouth opened, jaw moving up and down like a puppet. Crimson drool oozed down his chin.

Hizam moaned as he slid along the length of the desk. The major hit the floor. His vision blurred as he stared up at the ceiling. Something that resembled a fuzzy skull seemed to hover above him. Death, Hizam thought as he felt his life bleed away, is not as glorious as I expected.

Nyoka slashed his bayonet at the remaining Libyan. The terrorist leaped away from the blade and nearly tripped over the corpse of a slain comrade. The Libyan fell to one knee. His hand brushed the metal stock of the

AK-47. With a shout of triumph, he grabbed the rifle and swung it toward Nyoka.

A tidal wave of 9mm blitzers suddenly chopped into the Libyan's neck and shoulders. His head snapped to one side, blood jetting from a severed carotid. The fanatic slumped to the floor, his body twisting and convulsing in a macabre break dance of death.

Rafael Encizo stood at the doorway. Ribbons of smoke rose from the muzzle of his Uzi submachine gun. Nyoka stared at the Cuban as Encizo stepped across the threshold. The Phoenix Force commando glanced about the room, surprised to find it decorated with dead Libyans. Ambassador Mafuta stood behind his desk, hands raised in surrender.

"Looks like you hombres saved me some time," Encizo announced as he aimed the Uzi at Nyoka and squeezed the trigger.

Nothing happened. The weapon had jammed.

Nyoka charged, thrusting his bayonet at Encizo's belly. The Cuban parried the knife thrust with the frame of his Uzi and snared the sleeve above Nyoka's bayonet. The African shoved hard, driving Encizo back into the doorjamb.

The mercenary tried to ram a knee between Encizo's legs, but the Cuban shifted a leg to block the attack. Encizo stomped a boot heel into his opponent's instep. Nyoka cursed and struggled to pull his sleeve from the Cuban's grasp in order to use his bayonet.

Encizo smashed the frame of the Uzi into Nyoka's face. The African was knocked backward six feet, blood trickling from a split lip. Nyoka staggered to a stop, snarled with rage and hurled his bayonet at the Cuban.

The Phoenix Force warrior dodged to the right. The bayonet struck the doorjamb, the blade tip biting deep into wood. Nyoka's hand clawed at the Makarov pistol on his hip.

The Cuban swapped the Uzi from his right hand to his left and yanked a *shaken* from the strap of his shoulder holster. Encizo's arm swung as Nyoka drew his side arm. The Japanese throwing-star hurled into the African's chest, two tines stabbing flesh.

Nyoka screamed and stumbled two steps, stunned and startled by the stinging pain in his chest. The Russian autoloader was still in his fist. Nyoka's thumb hit the safety catch, but slipped against metal.

Encizo quickly lunged forward and chopped the barrel of his Uzi across his opponent's wrist. The Makarov fell to the floor. The Cuban grabbed the subgun in both hands and punted the steel frame into Nyoka's chest. The blow hammered the *shaken*, driving the tines deeper.

Nyoka was propelled backward by the blow. He collided with the desk and collapsed beside the corpse of Major Hizam. The African coughed, spitting blood. Then his body relaxed in the eternal calm of death.

Ambassador Mafuta had slipped from behind his desk during the fight. He darted for the door, panic-stricken and desperate. Yakov Katzenelenbogen met him at the doorway. The African came to an abrupt halt when he found himself staring into the Israeli's Uzi.

"Hello, Ambassador," Katz greeted with a smile. "We'd like to have a talk with you about foreign affairs."

"There's a bomb," Mafuta gasped. "We'll all be blown to bits...."

"Where is it?" McCarter demanded as he stood in the hall behind Katz.

"Down the hall," Mafuta replied, pointing a finger as he spoke. "Third door to the left."

The Briton dashed through the corridor to the third door and kicked it open. His Ingram machine pistol held ready, McCarter entered the room. A conference table had been shoved against a wall. Four large blocks of plastic explosives sat on the table top. Wires connected the detonators to a timing device.

"Jesus," McCarter rasped. He reckoned there was about eight pounds of plastique. Enough to blast a battleship into scrap metal.

Suddenly, the primitive battle cry of a jungle beast filled the room. McCarter whirled to confront the manlike creature leaping from the doorway, arms extended and leopard claws poised for attack.

Jino slashed both arms at the Briton. The claws raked McCarter's forearms, tearing cloth and cutting long furrows in flesh. The Phoenix Force ace gasped in pain as the machine pistol slipped from his grasp.

A leopard claw lashed at McCarter's face. The Briton ducked beneath the deadly swipe and hooked a fist under Jino's ribs. He punched his other hand into the leopard man's gut. Jino snarled and swung a backhand sweep at McCarter. The Englishman staggered back against the table, blood oozing from his ripped shirt.

Jino pounced, landing on McCarter like the cat he emulated. The Briton grabbed his opponent's forearms and held back the murderous claws. Jino hissed with rage, baring his fanglike teeth.

The African's head thrust forward, jaws snapping like a steel trap at McCarter's throat. The Briton recoiled from the nightmare creature. Jino opened his mouth wide and prepared to launch another bite, hoping to tear out McCarter's jugular with his teeth.

McCarter's head moved faster. The Briton rammed the front of his hard skull into the bridge of Jino's nose.

He followed the head-butt with a right cross to the terrorist's jaw, hitting his opponent as hard as he could.

Jino staggered away from McCarter. The Briton used the table for a brace as he pumped a boot into the African's chest. The kick sent Jino hurtling across the room. The fanatic connected with a wall and immediately lunged once more at his adversary.

Time was running out fast. McCarter reached for his Browning autoloader as the beast-man leaped forward. The Briton suddenly folded a leg and dropped to the floor, pulling the pistol from shoulder leather. Jino's hurtling form sailed over McCarter's prone body.

The Browning roared. Jino convulsed in midair as a 9mm parabellum slug smashed into his torso. The African crash-landed on the table beside the bomb. Jino clawed at the furniture and tried to drag his injured body into an attack position.

McCarter raised the Browning in a two-hand weaver's grip, aimed carefully, and shot the African between the eyes.

He rose unsteadily to his feet and leaned against the table. The Briton gazed down at the timer. Its dial was almost touching the zero point. McCarter's hands trembled as he reached for the wires connected to the explosives.

The bomb could be booby-trapped. One wrong move could detonate the explosives. Manning would know how to handle the situation, but the Canadian demolitions pro was not in the room with the bomb, and McCarter could not wait for Manning to arrive.

The Briton took a deep breath and grabbed the detonator wires. He closed his eyes and gritted his teeth together as he yanked hard. The wires were torn loose and the timer slipped off the table to the floor.

A harsh buzz sang from the device as the dial touched zero.

McCarter uttered a sigh of relief as he wiped the back of his hand across his sweat-covered brow.

20

The SAS commandos and Royal Marines outside the Mardarajan embassy stirred restlessly. The fighting within the building had stopped and everyone was eager to learn the outcome of the battle.

Colonel Katzenelenbogen gazed through the lenses of his M-17 gas mask as he stared out a window at the soldiers. He turned to Ambassador Mafuta. The African trembled as he stood with his hands cuffed behind his back.

"All right, *mon ami*," Katz began, addressing Mafuta in French, his voice distorted by the filters of his mask. "When we leave the building, you head straight for the soldiers and surrender. Tell them you want to talk to the television people. News reporters and camera crews from nine countries are waiting out there so you won't have any trouble getting an audience. *Comprenez?*"

"Oui, monsieur," Mafuta replied eagerly. "I will tell the truth. I will explain how the Libyans forced us to do these terrible things and how Mardaraja is just a puppet of Colonel Khaddafi. I owe them no loyalty and it will be a pleasure to expose this evil."

"Nobody will believe you're just an innocent bystander, Mafuta," McCarter muttered. He also spoke French and, like the other members of Phoenix Force, wore an M-17 mask as well. "But you're a little fish and nobody wants to crucify you. Just tell the truth."

"Is everybody ready?" Gary Manning asked, holding a small remote-control unit in his hand.

"As ready as we'll ever be," Calvin James answered.

"Let's get this over with, amigo," Encizo agreed.

Manning pressed a button. The remote transmitted a signal to the radio detonators connected to several tear-gas canisters positioned throughout the embassy. Great billows of green smoke immediately filled the building and poured through broken windowpanes.

Mafuta began to choke on the nauseous fumes, but Phoenix Force waited at the door of the embassy until enough gas had drifted outside to form a dense artificial fog. SAS and Royal Marines quickly donned gas masks as the green clouds drifted toward them.

"Now!" Katz declared, shoving Mafuta out the door.

The ambassador ran to a group of soldiers, waving his arms and pleading with them not to shoot him. Attention was naturally centered on Mafuta. Phoenix Force took advantage of the distraction. They crept through the green fog until they reached a group of SAS troops.

Dressed in SAS commando gear, the five adventurers mingled among the SAS strike force members undetected. They had discarded all weapons except their side arms to prevent suspicion as they headed toward a pair of armored cars parked by a curb.

"Hold up a moment," a tall waspy figure ordered through the filters of his own gas mask. "Where are you men off to?"

McCarter stiffened when he recognized the voice. The tall SAS officer moved in front of Phoenix Force and jammed his fists in his narrow hips. Major Simms narrowed his eyes behind the lenses of his mask, peering at the five men as if trying to see through the M-17 masks strapped to their faces.

"You blokes aren't wearing the unit shoulder patch," Simms declared. "What outfit are you with?"

"We're with Bravo, sir," McCarter replied, trying to disguise his voice and hoping that the filters of his M-17 would further distort it.

"Bravo?" Simms said doubtfully. He turned his head toward the embassy as if trying to find an answer there. Perhaps he did. "You chaps get the hell out of here. I'll see what I can do about keeping everybody else busy for a while."

"Thank you, sir," McCarter told him.

"Move your arse, mate," Simms ordered. "And good luck."

The major began barking orders at several of his men, sending them forward to cover the embassy in case any terrorists tried to sneak outside. He issued some similar demands to a few Royal Marines. When they hesitated, Simms announced that he wanted to speak to their bloody commanding officer immediately.

Phoenix Force easily slipped through the security net while the military bickered with each other and the press interviewed Ambassador Mafuta. The five-man army found a large green van parked by a tobacco shop. The back of the rig was unlocked. They climbed inside and bolted the door from within.

"My God," Felix Holmes remarked, peeking through a small window. The gunrunner was seated behind the steering wheel, smoking his tenth cigarette since he had been waiting in the van. "All five of you daft blokes made it back alive."

"Yeah," Gary Manning replied as he stripped off his gas mask. "But let's take a little drive outside of London for a while. Be nice to see some English countryside before we leave."

"Righto, mate," Holmes agreed cheerfully. "How'd everything turn out?"

"Mission accomplished," Katz informed him. "And it couldn't have turned out better."

A bonus for Phoenix Force readers:
Duel of Honor
Deep background on Keio Ohara,
Phoenix Force's fallen comrade

The four men sat in the brown leather armchairs surrounding a coffee table with several bottles of whisky, brandy and rum. They had congregated in the den at Gary Manning's home in Ontario. With tumblers filled with the alcoholic drink of their choice, Manning, Yakov Katzenelenbogen, David McCarter and Rafael Encizo saluted a fallen comrade at arms—Keio Ohara. They were all present at Ohara's wake. Only Calvin James, the newest member of Phoenix Force, was missing. He had not wished to intrude on their personal grief.

James had known Ohara only briefly, but he had quickly learned to respect the Japanese warrior. James had joined Phoenix Force at the beginning of the mission to stop the insidious Black Alchemist terrorists—the mission that would prove to be the last for Keio Ohara. Indeed, James had his share of grief, but it did not match the loss the others felt. The black man felt the wake was something special for the man who had fought side by side, so many times, with Ohara.

"By God," David McCarter began, his speech slurred by the amount of Scotch whisky he had consumed. "Keio showed those bastards."

"Yes, he did," Katzenelenbogen agreed. The Israeli was the only man who was not drunk. Katz never allowed himself that luxury. He had learned that grief is all too often a part of life and something that cannot be defeated by alcohol.

"Funny thing," Rafael Encizo said, pouring himself another glass of rum. "Since that business with his uncle, Keio seemed more at peace with himself than ever before."

"That incident was really something," Manning stated, fumbling for a bottle of brandy. "Keio sure handled that one like a . . . like a champ."

"Like a samurai," McCarter corrected. "And he sure as bloody hell didn't leave anything for us to do on that one. Remember?"

They remembered. It had happened not long after their return from a mission in Korea. . . .

KEIO OHARA kept an apartment in the "Little Tokyo" district of San Francisco. As he approached his front door, Ohara sensed danger. Since he was already on alert for a call to action for another Phoenix Force mission, Keio carried his .44 AutoMag in a briefcase. The Japanese member of Mack Bolan's foreign legion opened the case as he drew closer, glancing around to be certain no passersby were watching.

He stopped by the door when he saw what had triggered his sixth sense of survival. The door stood open an inch. Keio pulled the AutoMag from the valise and took a deep breath. He kicked the door open and entered the room in a spinning tumble. He shoulder-rolled across the floor and rose swiftly, the big steel pistol scanning for a target. The room was empty except for a still form on Keio's couch. Keio aimed the AutoMag at the figure but held his fire. It presented no threat. A sword had been driven into its chest.

Ohara quickly searched his apartment before turning on the lights. Then he examined the sinister figure on his couch. It was a mannequin, dressed in Ohara's own *kendo* uniform, the outfit worn by students of Japanese fencing. The vented *men* face mask covered the plastic features of the dummy. A note was pinned to the breast-plate by the long sword buried in the mannequin's chest.

Ohara's face tensed with anger when he recognized the sword. It was his own *katana*, the sword of his samurai ancestors, handed down from generation to generation. He was infuriated that this honored weapon, the very soul of the Ohara clan, had been used in such a manner.

He pulled the sword from the dummy and read the note. It was written in Japanese ideographs.

Nephew,
  I call upon you to face me as honor dictates—in a duel to the death. Your father and mother were responsible for my dishonor, and you were witness to the disgrace of my exile from the clan. Recently you and four others terminated my employer in Hawaii. This has contributed to a blood debt that must be settled. If the Code of Bushido still has any meaning for you, you shall face me alone. I await you at Alcatraz Island.

                                                                 Teko

Indeed, Ohara recalled Teko's expulsion from the family clan. Teko was Keio's uncle, the elder of two brothers. Thus, by virtue of his birthright, Teko was to succeed his father as head of the clan. However, Teko had fallen in with *yakuza* criminals after World War II. This was a disgrace to the Ohara family. Keio's grandfather had assembled the family at the dojo hall of the Shimato temple in Kyoto to witness Teko's shame.

Teko was stripped of his birthright and his name was no longer to be uttered by the Ohara clan. But Teko challenged the decision. He demanded a duel of honor with his successor. Keio's father, Toshiro Ohara, accepted the challenge.

The brothers, armed with *katana* fighting swords, faced each other. Toshiro held the traditional weapon of the Ohara clan. The fight was over in scant seconds. Cut in many places, Teko lay bleeding on the tatami mat. He dragged himself in shame from the temple. He was never mentioned by the Ohara family or heard from again. Until now.

Keio Ohara could not refuse Teko's challenge, just as his father could not have refused to duel fifteen years earlier on that fateful night at the Shimato temple. It was a matter of honor. Phoenix Force, Stony Man and the President of the United States would have to wait until this personal matter had been paid in full with blood. Either Teko's or Keio's blood.

Ohara scribbled a note and put it next to his phone. He could not notify the other members of Phoenix Force. He would have to face his corrupt uncle alone, but if he did not return, at least the others would know why.

Ohara retrieved his briefcase from the hall and prepared for battle. He donned a black night-camouflage suit and a pair of split-toe *tabi* boots with rubber soles, a modern version of the footgear worn by *ninja* espionage agents and assassins. The .44 AutoMag went into a hip holster, and four extra magazines were loaded into ammo pouches on his belt. He cleaned and sharpened the honored *katana* and returned it to its scabbard before inserting the sword into a carrying case. Ohara packed a grappling hook and rope and added a pouch of *shaken* throwing stars to his belt. He packed his gear in an innocent-looking U.S. Army duffel bag and headed for his car.

Although anxious to get to Alcatraz, Ohara held his natural *kamikaze* driving instincts in check and drove slowly and carefully to the waterfront. He parked the car and donned his weaponry. Then Ohara slipped into the shadows, becoming one with the night.

Within minutes, Ohara located a small boat tied to the end of a wharf. He slipped it free and began rowing toward the most escape-proof prison ever built. The Rock. Alcatraz. The island, with its collection of buildings, jutted from the water like a clenched fist with a concrete cestus around its knuckles.

As Keio rowed out to the bay, a shadowy figure on the docks watched, nodding with satisfaction. The man spoke into a transceiver.

"He is on his way, Ohara-*sama*," he said, squinting into the night. The small boat could no longer be seen from the dock.

"Good, Matsu-*san*," the voice of Teko Ohara replied from the radio. "Return to Tiger Base Alpha and await further instructions."

Keio Ohara continued to row toward Alcatraz. In his note, Teko had mentioned an "employer in Hawaii." That could only refer to Professor Edward Oshimi, and the connection suggested that Teko had become a terrorist as well as a criminal; Keio's uncle would have little concern for the Code of Bushido. There could be a small army of killers waiting at the island. Ohara accepted this risk. To face his uncle in combat was his duty for more reasons than one.

Ohara's father and mother had been killed in a car accident earlier that year. Ken Ikeda, a Kompei Intelligence agent in Tokyo who had formerly worked with Phoenix Force, had contacted Ohara.

"Our lab people checked the car wreck, Ohara-*san*," Ikeda explained. "They discovered the brake lines and steering cable had been cut. Someone murdered your parents, my friend.''

Keio Ohara had blamed himself for the deaths of his father and mother, certain that an enemy of Phoenix Force had struck at them as a way of revenge. Could it be that Teko had been responsible? If so, Keio Ohara was about to fight the most important battle of his life. Regardless of the odds, he would have to face Teko. If he avenged his parents murder, this would be karma. If he died, this too would be karma.

At last Ohara reached the island. He blended with the darkness as he crept to the outer wall of Alcatraz prison. No longer used to hold convicts in cells, the Rock had become a tourist site with only a small security force on hand. The guards would be no match for a group of professional terrorists. Teko could indeed have seized control of the entire island without much trouble.

Ohara hurled the grappling hook. The rubber-coated blades struck the rim of the wall. The hook silently caught and held. The Japanese warrior scaled the wall, pulling himself up the rope, hand over hand, his *tabi*-clad feet braced against concrete.

A mild breeze was blown in from the Pacific into San Francisco Bay. Light tendrils of fog quested through the darkness as Ohara reached the top of the wall. He spotted the first guard. The terrorist marched along a catwalk, his back turned to the Phoenix Force commando. Ohara reached into a pouch and hurled a *shaken*. It struck the terrorist behind the right ear, a sharp tine puncturing skull and brain. The guard felt as if he had been stung by a giant mosquito. It was the last sensation he experienced.

Ohara moved on. He made a quick probe of the area, trying to determine how large a force he was up against.

It was impossible to estimate the strength of his enemy, but he was now certain that his evil uncle was not alone. After a brief stop at each guard tower, Ohara descended to the lower levels.

WITHIN THE PRISON, Teko Ohara sat cross-legged on the floor in the middle of the great cell block. He was dressed in a black kimono jacket and *hakama*, a *katana* fighting sword close at him.

Soon his nephew would arrive. Teko sensed this. He had prepared for this night. Teko had trained zealously for many years to hone his martial-arts skills in kendo and karate. Although not a tall man, Teko was powerfully built, his body a mass of muscles without an ounce of fat. He was certain he would be more than a match for Keio, who had become a lackey for the Western barbarians.

Following the destruction of Professor Oshimi's operation in Hawaii, Teko had been one of the few terrorists involved to escape with his life. Fortunately for the renegade, he and a handful of others had been at the island of Lanai when Phoenix Force attacked Oshimi's stronghold.

Since then, Teko had devoted himself to his own criminal and terrorist pursuits. And to settling his score with his own family. Toshiro, his brother, had already paid with his life. Now only Keio remained. The final debt would be paid in blood that night.

Teko gathered up his sword and prepared to receive his nephew.

KEIO OHARA crept across the huge exercise yard. Suddenly the brilliant beam of a spotlight flashed on, pinning him like a moth to a display board. Five opponents rushed at him from various corners of the yard. One carried a Mini-24 semiautomatic rifle, another held a pump shotgun and the other three brandished pistols. They held their fire, obviously hoping to take Ohara alive.

The Phoenix Force warrior was not going to make it easy for his assailants. The big steel AutoMag appeared in his fist. Orange flame streaked from the muzzle as the powerful pistol roared. A .44 Magnum slug punched through the chest of the man with the rifle, cutting him down before he could use his Mini-14.

Ohara had picked off the rifleman first because the weapon with the greatest range was the greatest threat. The other four terrorists opened fire as they ran, but their pistols lacked the impressive range and accuracy of Ohara's AutoMag. Bullets plucked earth near the warrior's feet as he blasted another .44 round through the upper torso of a second opponent.

The shotgun bellowed. Pellets tore up the ground behind Ohara. He whirled and triggered his AutoMag again. The big projectile smashed into the shotgunner's forehead and exploded most of his skull into a geyser of crimson and gray slime.

A pistol bullet stung Ohara's right thigh. The hot slug cut cloth and creased flesh. The Phoenix Force pro dropped to the ground and fired his weapon from a prone position. A fourth terrorist was sent to his private hell by a .44 Magnum round through the heart.

More bullets struck the earth near Ohara. Some of these came from snipers positioned on the wall. Obviously more terrorists had already climbed to the elevated vantage point. Ohara shifted around, aimed and fired. The spotlight burst apart and darkness reclaimed the exercise yard.

A voice cried out in alarm, startled by the sudden darkness. Ohara fired at the sound. Another scream responded as the terrorist fell in a dying heap. Snipers fired at Ohara, aiming at the muzzle-flash of his AutoMag. The Japanese warrior bolted, firing back at the enemy riflemen.

Ohara ejected the spent magazine from his weapon as he ran and reached for another mag. Another spotlight flooded harsh illumination across the yard. Ohara found himself face to face with a large Oriental who was also trying to reload a handgun. The terrorist slashed his pistol at Ohara, striking the AutoMag from the Phoenix Force crusader's grasp.

Ohara's leg shot out, driving a foot-sword kick to his adversary's abdomen. The man doubled up with a gasp, and Ohara snapped a backfist to the terrorist's face. The man staggered, shook his head and launched a high roundhouse kick at the commando's head. Ohara ducked beneath the hurtling foot and thrust a dragon's head punch between his opponent's legs.

The middle knuckle of his fist smashed into a testicle, bursting it like a cherry bomb. The terrorist shrieked in agony and wilted to the ground. Another rifle snarled from the wall. The bullet narrowly missed Ohara and struck the disabled thug, drilling a lethal tunnel through his face.

Ohara dived to the ground and rolled as snipers continued to fire at him. The Phoenix Force champion reached the Mini-14 discarded by a slain opponent. He braced the rifle against a hip and triggered it, pointing the weapon at the second spotlight. Two 5.56mm rounds smashed the light and plunged the yard into darkness once more.

Ohara's left hand found a small radio transmitter on his belt. He pressed a button to send a special ultrahigh frequency to the radio detonators planted in the C-4 plastic explosive packets he had left in each guard tower.

The tower exploded. Chunks of concrete and shredded, mangled corpses hurled in all directions. Parts of the wall came tumbling down as if Joshua had returned to take on a modern-day Jericho. Ohara retreated to the nearest doorway, the Mini-14 in his fists.

Time was running out. The explosions would alert the harbor patrol and the SFPD would soon be sending a SWAT team to Alcatraz. Ohara would be lucky to get away before the police arrived. He would be lucky if he survived his one-man assault on his uncle's terrorist camp, period.

Finding himself in the main cell block, Ohara crept along the great corridor, scanning the dimly lit interior, searching for terrorists.

Something moved overhead. Ohara glanced up to see a shotgun-wielding figure lean over the railing of a tier. He snap-aimed the Mini-14 and squeezed the trigger twice. Two 55-grain projectiles sliced through the gunman like an icepick through rice paper. The terrorist collapsed, his corpse draped over the rail.

"Haaii-yaa!" a voice cried as a sword-swinging figure burst forward and charged Ohara.

The Phoenix Force pro hesitated, his finger poised on the trigger. He thought the attacker might be his uncle. Ohara wanted to face Teko with the family *katana* in hand. A bullet would not be a fitting end for the treacherous renegade.

The swordsman was not Teko Ohara, but he was well schooled in the art of kendo. The terrorist's sword slashed like a bolt of lightning. Ohara raised the Mini-14 to parry to the blade. The impact of the *katana* against the barrel ripped the rifle from Ohara's hands. He jumped back and drew his own *katana* in a single swift motion.

The enemy swordsman raised his weapon in a two-hand grip and executed an overhead *shominuch* stroke. Ohara's *katana* parried the attack, the flat of his sword deflecting the terrorist's blade. Then he thrust both arms forward, lunging the slanted point of his *katana* into the aggressor's face.

Sharp steel lanced the terrorist's right eyeball. The man screamed as the point pierced into his eye socket and punctured the brain. The terrorist dropped his sword. Ohara pulled the blade of his *katana* from the guy's blood-streaked face and watched his corpse drop to the floor.

Without warning, sharp steel slashed Ohara's back. Fortunately his body was already moving and the treacherous attack sliced cloth and only cut a shallow wound between his shoulder blades, narrowly missing his spine. Ohara leaped forward and spun around to face Teko Ohara. His uncle held a *katana* in his fists, a crimson stain along its razor edge.

"So, dog son of my accursed brother—" Teko spat the words with bitter hatred "—I trust you are ready to join your ancestors. Especially your worthless father and the diseased whore who gave birth to you."

"I have done as honor demanded and come to meet you for the duel, nameless one," Ohara replied grimly, trying to control his anger, aware that losing his temper would be more apt to make him careless—something Teko was no doubt hoping for.

"Do you realize that I killed your precious father and your slut mother, nephew?" Teko asked with a cruel smile.

"You were wise not to try to fight my father again," Keio replied simply. "But you should have arranged an accident for me, as well. That is a mistake which will now cost you your life, dog vomit."

"We'll see who dies, you impudent pup!" screamed

Teko as he leaped forward, delivering an overhead stroke with his *katana*.

Keio blocked the attack with the flat of his own sword. Teko suddenly pivoted and hooked a forward elbow smash to Ohara's face. Keio staggered from the blow, tasting blood. Teko's sword slashed a quick backhand sweep, slicing a diagonal cut across his nephew's belly.

Ohara backed away, his *katana* held ready. Blood trickled from a gash in his abdomen, but he did not retreat when Teko charged once more. The renegade swung another overhead stroke at the younger man, trying to split Keio's skull like a melon.

Ohara blocked the deadly stroke, but Teko shoved hard, trying to slide his sword into a stabbing position. The Phoenix Force warrior suddenly folded a leg and dropped backward, pulling his tormentor forward. Keio's back touched the floor and his right foot caught Teko in the abdomen. The renegade cried out as his nephew straightened his leg to send Teko hurtling overhead in a judo circle-throw.

Teko crashed to the floor and scurried upright, his *katana* in hand. Keio Ohara waited for his uncle to attack again. The renegade feinted another *shominuch* stroke, then suddenly attempted a thrust for Keio's stomach.

Ohara nimbly sidestepped, raising his sword as he moved. Teko's weapon stabbed air. Ohara's *katana* descended swiftly in a *sodesuri* cut. The terrorist screamed as sharp steel sliced his left wrist to the bone. Teko bellowed in rage and delivered a cross-body sweep, holding the sword in his right hand. Keio parried the attack and jabbed his sword at Teko's neck.

Teko dodged his nephew's *katana*, but the stroke was a feint. Ohara suddenly spun, dropped low and delivered a *tabigata* attack, slashing his uncle's right leg. The terrorist shrieked and leaped back into the barred door of a cell. Half blind with pain, Teko still raised his *katana* and struck out once more.

Ohara quickly shuffled forward and raised his sword, thrusting the sharp steel into the path of Teko's arm. The terrorist's own momentum slammed his right wrist against the *katana*'s unyielding edge. He screamed as flesh and bone were severed. His fist, still clenched to the haft of his sword, fell by Teko's feet as blood fountained from the stump of his wrist.

Keio Ohara stepped back and stared at his bloodied, helpless opponent. There was nothing left to do except finish off Teko once and forever. He slashed a fast *nino-do* stroke across the terrorist's belly. Teko doubled up, scarlet gushing from his ripped stomach. Ohara delivered one last sword stroke, cutting into the back of Teko's neck, slicing vertebrae like old cheese. The renegade's head tumbled across the floor as his decapitated corpse slid against the cell door, trembling in a muscular spasm as if unwilling to accept death.

Only then did Keio Ohara notice the gunfire coming from outside the cell block. He turned toward the doorway as two familiar figures appeared. Yakov Katzenelenbogen held a smoking Uzi submachine gun braced across his prosthetic right arm, and David McCarter had his pet Ingram M-10 held ready. The Phoenix Force pair raised their weapons to point at the ceiling as they noticed Ohara was the only figure still alive in the corridor.

"Not only does this bloke have a party without inviting us," McCarter began, glancing down at Teko's mutilated corpse, "he has to go and serve up cold cuts, as well."

Keio smiled at his friend's black humor. "I assume you found my letter?"

"We found it," Katz said, nodding. "We came as soon as David could get his hands on a helicopter. Not that you needed us. We found a couple wounded idiots outside who still had some fight left in them, but it appears the real battle was in here."

Keio Ohara wiped his uncle's blood from the blade of his honored *katana* and slid the sword into its scabbard. At last he had avenged the deaths of his father and mother. He had done so with pride and honor. Rest well, my parents, Ohara thought. For the first time since he had learned of the murder of his father and mother, Keio Ohara was at peace with himself.

AND NOW PHOENIX FORCE remembered their Japanese comrade-at-arms in the quiet and security of Gary Manning's den. They raised their glasses for a final toast.

"To Keio Ohara," Rafael Encizo said, his tongue heavy from too much rum, "the bravest warrior we have known. A true samurai."

The others nodded in agreement and downed their drinks. Katz, the only sober man in the room, rose and faced the others.

"We'd better get some sleep, gentlemen," the Israeli declared. "It won't be long before we'll have another mission. That's the way of the world, you know."

Indeed, it would not be long before Phoenix Force would again be summoned to the hellgrounds once again. The never-ending struggle against the forces of terrorism would soon beckon them to a new front. That was the way it would always be. Until at last there was no longer a need for warriors to protect the innocent from the savages.

The warrior fire would continue to burn until then.

And Phoenix Force would keep the fire burning.

Mack Bolan's

PHOENIX FORCE

by Gar Wilson

Schooled in guerilla warfare, equipped with all the latest lethal hardware, Phoenix Force battles the powers of darkness in an endless crusade for freedom, justice and the rights of the individual. Follow the adventures of one of the legends of the genre. Phoenix Force is the free world's foreign legion!

"The new heroes of the eighties that America has been waiting for."

—Gary S. Roen, *Orlando Voice*

Phoenix Force titles are available wherever paperbacks are sold.

GOLD EAGLE

Mack Bolan's

ABLE TEAM

by Dick Stivers

Action writhes in the reader's own street as Able Team's Carl "Mr. Ironman" Lyons, Pol Blancanales and Gadgets Schwarz make triple trouble in blazing war. To these superspecialists, justice is as sharp as a knife. Join the guys who began it all—Dick Stivers's Able Team!

"This guy has a fertile mind and a great eye for detail. Dick Stivers is brilliant!"

—*Don Pendleton*

Able Team titles are available wherever paperbacks are sold.

GOLD
EAGLE

GET THE
NEW WAR BOOK
AND MACK BOLAN
BUMPER STICKER <u>FREE</u>!
Mail this coupon today!

FREE! <u>THE NEW WAR BOOK</u> AND MACK BOLAN BUMPER STICKER
when you join our home subscription plan.

Gold Eagle Reader Service, a division of Worldwide Library
In U.S.A.: 2504 W. Southern Avenue, Tempe, Arizona 85282
In Canada: P.O. Box 2800, Postal Station A, 5170 Yonge Street, Willowdale, Ont. M2N 6J3

YES, rush me <u>The New War Book</u> and Mack Bolan bumper sticker FREE, and, under separate cover, my first six Gold Eagle novels. These first six books are mine to examine free for 10 days. If I am not entirely satisfied with these books, I will return them within 10 days and owe nothing. If I decide to keep these novels, I will pay just $1.95 per book (total $11.70). I will then receive the six Gold Eagle novels every other month, and will be billed the same low price of $11.70 per shipment. I understand that each shipment will contain two Mack Bolan novels, and one each from the Able Team, Phoenix Force, SOBs and Track libraries. There are no shipping and handling or any other hidden charges. I may cancel this arrangement at any time, and <u>The New War Book</u> and bumper sticker are mine to keep as gifts, even if I do not buy any additional books.

IMPORTANT BONUS: If I continue to be an active subscriber to Gold Eagle Reader Service, you will send me FREE, with every shipment, the AUTOMAG newsletter as a FREE BONUS!

Name	(please print)

Address	Apt. No.

City	State/Province	Zip/Postal Code

Signature   (If under 18, parent or guardian must sign.)

This offer limited to one order per household. We reserve the right to exercise discretion in granting membership. If price changes are necessary you will be notified.
116–BPM–PAE5

AA-SUB-1R

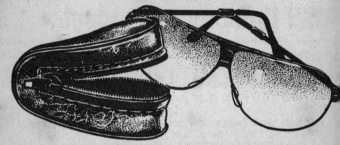